SUDDENLY THE MINOTAUR

MARIE HÉLÈNE POITRAS

SUDDENLY THE MINOTAUR

TRANSLATED BY PATRICIA CLAXTON

Cover illustration by Josée Bisaillon.
Author photograph by John Lodoño.
Book designed and typeset by Primeau & Barey, Montreal.
Printed and bound in Canada by Marquis Imprimeur.
Interior pages printed on 100 per cent recycled and
FSC certified Rolland Enviro 100 paper.
Distributed by Lit DistCo.

Legal Deposit, *Bibliothèque et Archives nationales du Québec*
and the National Library of Canada, 4th trimester, 2006.

Library and Archives Canada Cataloguing in Publication
Poitras, Marie Hélène, 1975-
[Soudain le Minotaure. English]
Suddenly the Minotaur/Marie Hélène Poitras;
translated by Patricia Claxton.
Translation of: Soudain le Minotaure.
ISBN-10: 1-897190-16-6 ISBN-13: 978-1-897190-16-6 (pbk.)
ISBN-10: 1-897190-17-4 ISBN-13: 978-1-897190-17-3 (bound)
I. Claxton, Patricia, 1929- II. Title.
III. Title: Soudain le Minotaure. English.
PS8581.O245S6813 2006 C843'.6
C2006-905434-7

For our publishing activities, DC Books gratefully acknowledges
the financial support of The Canada Council for the Arts, of SODEC,
and of the Government of Canada through the Book Publishing
Industry Development Program (BPIDP).

Canada Council for the Arts Conseil des Arts du Canada

Société de développement des entreprises culturelles

DC Books
PO Box 666, Station Saint-Laurent
Montreal, Quebec H4L 4V9
www.dcbooks.ca

I dedicate this novel to
Pierre Lepage, a tanned angel
playing tennis in heaven.

With thanks to
André Carpentier
and Nancy Hall.

CONTENTS

TRANSLATOR'S NOTE

A good translation, it is generally assumed, accurately reproduces the words contained in the original work. But as Sportin' Life said about Jonas and the Whale, it ain't necessarily so. Different languages are constructed differently and work differently with the words at their disposal, even when there are some shared roots and words that look comfortingly similar. Moreover, authors have their own sense of words and their own ways of putting those words together.

I have worked closely with Marie Hélène Poitras to make sure her intentions are accurately reflected in this translation. She has paid close attention and raised some questions that have led to changes in the translation, and the translation process has raised some that have led to changes in the underlying work. An example of the first is the fact that a *pomélo* is not a grapefruit but a related citrus fruit which in English is called a "shaddock" or "pomelo." Also, after explanation of the intent concerning dreams that are *logés en abyme dans le sommeil,* this more difficult concept yields the phrase "[dreams] that are innate in sleep." One of the few original text corrections arises from Marie Hélène's own observation that the Queen's likeness does not in fact appear on the Canadian $5 bill, or on the $10, but does on the $20 bill. Another amends the *Croix de David* in the Dachau cemetery to the "Star of David." Occasional slight modifications clarify the author's intent or rectify unintended contradiction or inconsistency.

The French book states that an apartment is *noir de suie. Suie* is "soot," but I was puzzled why the apartment should be "black with soot" until Marie Hélène explained that the *suie* is used as fingerprint material. I went on research. In the family of black fingerprint powders (of which there are eight), the most common are graphite and lampblack, and *suie* is obviously the second. It would be redundant and also puzzling for the English text to read, "black with lampblack," so this becomes, "grimy with lampblack fingerprint powder."

The name "Ariane," which is familiar in French-speaking societies, would translate as "Ariadne," which is not at all familiar as a given name in English and is rather ponderous, contrary to the phonetic and rhythmic lightness of "Ariane." The mythological link is important, but so is the tone imparted by the name. It was decided that "Ariane" should remain unchanged in the English translation.

Mino refers to his mother and father as *maman* and *papa* in the French book. Since he speaks French as well as Spanish, this is not out of place, but English is a language that is totally foreign to him and to have him refer to his parents as "Mom" and "Dad" (or some such) seems really incongruous, particularly in view of his use of numerous Spanish words in italic. In this English book, he therefore refers to his parents in Spanish as *mamá* and *papá.*

A translator's duties include attention to style and stylistic effect. Effect achieved by the author, of course, but also to things like unwanted effects owing to language differences. For example, there is a string of sentences beginning with *je* in French that do not lend themselves to combination. The same string of sentences beginning with the English "I," which is phonetically stronger and more intrusive with repetition, gives an unpleasant result that is not present in French. The solution is to change the syntax somewhere, perhaps only once, to break the displeasing sequence and restore a balance.

Changing the syntax–the order of words or groups of words–is in fact a translator's prerogative and often the key to clarity in expressing ideas in the language of translation. There is no reason to expect two languages to link ideas in the same order.

I have paid careful attention to the characters' language registers. Mino is interesting because what education he has had was through literature. His speech can be rough but, in contemplative and dream sequences especially, his private expression is literary, sometimes surrealistic. Ariane, the university student of literature, is young and does not talk like a grammar book; while her contemplation and dreaming are also literary, they are closer to reality than Mino's, even at the pinnacle of fear.

I would like to thank Marie Hélène Poitras for her enthusiastic and generous cooperation, and Josianne Le Guellec for some terminological assistance. I would also like to thank Steve Luxton and Keith Henderson of our publishers, DC Books.

Patricia Claxton
August, 2006

PART ONE
MINO TORRÈS

CHAPTER 1

The only girl I've seen in six months is the nurse. A giant, twice as big as me. She checks my vital signs every day. I'd sure like to pull her underpants over my head. She always looks me in the eye from way up there, and I'm pink and naked, a wad of gum waiting for her heel to come down on. I'm supposed to take off my clothes and wait till she comes into the room. It's always a long time. She's on the other side of the door laughing with one of the doctors, sometimes very hard, a coarse, unnecessarily loud laugh. No doubt she wants me to hear her, wants me to know she's really enjoying herself while I'm lying on the paper-covered bed, shivering, like a foetus in a garbage can.

From the other side of the two-way mirror, the nurse can see me take off my prison uniform, I know that perfectly well. I tell myself she's not interested, she must like women, she doesn't even look at me. But when I remove my underwear her loud laugh gets to me. Then she comes in with tears in her eyes still from laughing so much. She stares at me with a dumb look and pulls on plastic gloves that smell like condoms. Next she takes a little wooden paddle and orders me to stick out my tongue and say "aaah." She leans her fat bosom against my throat, and to keep my penis from standing up I think about my mother or a field of sugar cane. I haven't been able to get it up for the last two weeks anyway; Dr. Parker is giving me pills to tone down my sex urges.

I often have a dream that's the same every time. The prison corridors are empty. All the prisoners are sleeping a medicated sleep and their mouths are dry. By lucky chance, the guards have forgotten to bolt the door of my cell. I'm not escaping; I'm waiting for Nurse Smith. Distant sounds of heavy heels, powerful walk, and clinking keys. It's her. I can smell her cigarette and the sour stench of her armpits. She peers inside my cell and asks why I'm not asleep. I push the door open hard so it hits her in the face. She falls, stunned for a few seconds, and I climb on her before she comes to. I hold her wrists firmly with one hand and tear at her clothes with the keys until I can see her great flabby breasts and her greying crotch. I thrust between her bovine thighs. She gasps, groans, and comes, the corridor lights flash on and off wildly. We fall in love, we leave the detention centre and get in her car, a little forest-green Rabbit that's all rusty. I drive while she sews up her torn pants and we talk about driving on down as far as Virginia. She offers me a Marlboro.

CHAPTER 2

Mamá telephoned this morning. She thinks I'm making a respectable living here. My sister has just turned sixteen and for two months has been going with a thirty-year-old man who works in a bank and makes a good salary. In a voice that shows I care, I tell my mother to beware of this. She hands the receiver to Anna.

"Little sister, you better look out for yourself. I don't want anything to happen to you."

I'm afraid for her. She doesn't know anything about men yet and sometimes dresses provocatively. She wears tight t-shirts with plunging necklines that display her cleavage. Her butt's wrapped in short skirts that show the cheeks of her ass when she bends over to dig in her handbag.

I raped at least twenty girls in Guatemala. One of them went to the police, but they never found me. I'd been surprised how easy it was. As if the girls were expecting to be attacked sooner or later. It would all happen very fast. Wavy hair halfway down their backs. Swinging hips. My hand on their mouths. Their eyes all creamy with two coffee beans in the cream. I wanted to use more force with them but they gave in. The terror in their eyes elated me. I wanted to drink them, around us everything seemed to distend in slow sequences. I'd be raping them and they'd be making love to me. I'd wet their bellies with my sperm. I'd spit on their heads, like to make them dirty. Then I'd run off, promising myself I'd do it again. Taking them that way made me euphoric. The first time, I wore a Mickey Mouse mask. Hallowe'en was coming up.

A few days following that rape, I was upset by an article in the local paper reporting the event. After a day at the main market selling fruit, I came home a bit earlier than usual with a pack of American cigarettes and two mangoes for Anna.

Mamá wasn't there. My sister had skipped school like she often did when *Mamá* wasn't there, and had brought home three little punks older than her. A bottle of rum was open on the table. The radio was blaring American pop music, Madonna, I think. My sister was dancing with her arms in the air, which made it so you could very clearly see the cheeks of her ass. I watched the scene through the window for several minutes. The guys were putting away the brown booze straight from the bottle, ogling Anna's body as she turned round and round. She seemed to be a little drunk. The guys kept whispering things in each others' ears and now and then poured some rum in the bottle cap and held it out to Anna. She drank very quickly and they cheered her on. There was rape in the air, you could smell it.

I went in hollering and punched one of the guys. A pen-knife fell out of his pocket. He picked it up and ran to catch up with the other two. Anna lit into me, swearing, accusing me of never letting her have any fun, with her eyes flashing, yelling that she wasn't doing anything wrong. I bopped her on the head with the newspaper, not too hard, just to wound her pride and shut her up finally.

"You don't read the newspaper?"

"What's the newspaper got to do with it? And anyway, you took it with you this morning."

She was drunker than I'd thought at first. I lit her a cigarette and then showed her the article about the rape.

She stopped her yappy wailing.

On the telephone, my mother cries and tells me again she's proud of me and is happy to know things are going well. She thinks I'm working for a big Quebec company; she asks how Maria's doing. Hearing my own language, spoken by my mother besides, is like a caress to me. She wants to know when she's going to be a grandmother and tells me to hurry up or Anna will have children before I do. With a big belly, Anna would show halfway up her ass with her skirts. But I wouldn't ever rape a pregnant woman.

"Your mother's getting old, son."

I haven't been listening for a while.

"*Mamá,* I have to go. I have to get back to work."

And I go back to my cell, Number 303 at the Penetanguishene Detention Centre.

CHAPTER 3

Three nights in row, I went to the university at the corner of Saint-Denis and De Maisonneuve to watch the student girls go by. They were all very pretty, apart from some fat ones and some big ones in tracksuits with fuzz on their upper lips. I would sit at a table on the first floor mezzanine and look down at the students gathered round a fountain below. A terrible urge to fuck turned my stomach upside down. You can find what you want in a girl. If a man wants to rape her, she gives him the idea she's good only for that. That she's expecting it, even.

My wife never had an orgasm and always lay like a corpse while we had sex. I seemed to be emptying myself into a bag of organs. She didn't give a damn about not coming because the only reason she let me have her was she wanted to become a mommy. She got bored, alone in the apartment. Everything was always very clean. She wrapped the lamps in transparent plastic bags so they wouldn't get covered in dust. She wanted to take care of a child, give her breast to someone else but me. I sold fruits and vegetables at Jean-Talon Market, and we lived in an apartment in the North End of Montreal.

The city was beautiful in autumn. I'd bought coats for Maria and me. She only went outside with me. We'd go to the market and she'd choose fruits and vegetables, fish and meat, while I waited in a small café and read the paper. She would smile with happiness to have found citrus fruits from her home country, Costa Rica. I had told her that the city was dangerous for a woman alone and it was better if she didn't go out without me. Maria was very pretty, taller than me, with full lips, a golden complexion, and long black hair. I knew she attracted attention and smiles. I could have been taken for her younger brother and it annoyed me.

On a red October Monday, I came home from work around supper time. We'd been in Quebec since September. Maria had been to the hairdresser. Alone. Her long hair was lying in a box in the middle of the kitchen table, in a single braid attached at each end by a red bow. On her head, a tom-boy cut. A trickle of saliva was dribbling from her mouth; she had fallen asleep on the living room sofa watching a children's program. I kicked at all the walls and left the apartment. I had to get moving or I was in for an epileptic seizure. When I felt one coming on, I'd start running and sometimes I could save myself from it. I jumped in a bus, didn't matter which. When I got out I was in the Gay Village and I ran to get out of there as fast as I could. When I got to the *Université du Québec,* I knew I was going to commit another rape soon, and there'd be plenty of others and I'd pick girls with long hair.

CHAPTER 4

I stay curled up in the corner of my cell while the other prisoners play billiards or cards in the common room. Guys who take girls by force get themselves beaten up by other inmates and the guards have to isolate them. There are three of us rapist neighbours, digesting our mashed potatoes and our anti-erection pills and not being able to jerk off any more, which is all there is to do inside these grey walls. I count my teeth, run water from the tap over my face and scratch my ears while I wait for the next group therapy session.

Dr. Parker is knocking himself out telling us over and over that we're sick. I tell him we're sick because of all the pills he's giving us. The other prisoners chuckle. I'm the clown of the group, and we all think Parker's a doddering old fool. One inmate adds that the pills raise his voice a whole octave. The only thing I'm learning here is English. I think in Spanish, in French too, but I have to speak English. I'm uprooted even in my language.

At times I think about the girls I've raped. When I took the time to choose (maybe seven times out of ten), they would be slim, pretty, delicate, in a hurry, with long hair hanging down their backs, lower than their bra-fasteners, or pulled up in a knot on their heads, gazing up at the sky, letting their white cheeks show. None of them reacted the same way when I approached them, but they were all very frightened. Like some horrible animal was getting ready to gobble them up. I've raped exactly thirty-three girls, thirteen of them in Quebec. In my head they go by in no special order, like a chain of little cardboard figures joined at the arms. Two of them were virgins, friends of my sister's. I don't like it when they cry too much. There was that girl who was picking flowers not far from me, too, who was reading *Zorro.* I told her I knew a pretty place so full with roses that they would be picking her. She laughed. Her body was like a sky filled with beauty spots for stars and she had mauve nipples. One dumb broad was watching *tortugas* leaving the sea to lay their eggs on the beach. In a bathing suit, with her long legs. Alone in the dark at night. I call that an official invitation to rape. A gazelle that cuddles against a lion's ass to sleep and is surprised to wake up being eaten. Then there was that girl who smiled at me when she was buying melons. In Montreal, it was nearly always students that I dragged into lanes. There are several I forget. But I remember Ariane perfectly.

I thought Ariane would be at the trial. She's the only one whose name haunts me. I was able to get inside her apartment and wait for her because the doors weren't locked. I wiped my feet on the coco-fibre mat and explored the rooms. A guy was living with her, I could tell from the pictures of girls pinned up on the walls of one of the bedrooms. I found out Ariane's name from several expired student cards in the top left-hand drawer of her dresser. In a strip of three pictures taken in a shopping mall photo booth, two teens were mugging for the camera. I quickly recognized Ariane although the pictures were old; she was on the left and had a blue tongue. I don't know why. The fourth picture was torn off. Perhaps her friend had kept it.

I hid in the closet and waited for her. At last, footsteps on the stairs. A woman's voice murmuring something. It's her. I changed my mind and slipped behind the bedroom door. Then, no, that wasn't it; I went back to the closet. I think she was looking for her cat in the stairwell. The soft plop of a coat being dropped on the floor. The clunk of a set of keys being tossed on a table. A plastic bag being squished into a ball. I could already feel the adrenaline spreading through my spinal cord; I was going to have the courage to do it. Then Ariane came in, calling to a guy.

"François, are you here?"

I nearly killed her with my fingers. She's the only one who tried to get away. To have defended herself. Ariane was not going to get away from me. I hit her, I made her bleed, I wanted her to be afraid. At last I could do what I was doing with violence, I had no choice. Ariane, the only one whose name I know. I hoped she'd be at the trial because, even though I'd been rough with her, it seemed to me she might have understood. She might even have had a little compassion for me. Unfortunately it was the other one, the last one, whose boyfriend I stabbed, who turned up with her whole family. She came and spat in my face. A real dumb broad, that one.

CHAPTER 5

It must be early, 5 in the morning, I'd say. I think about Maria, my urban Bohemian, that tall, fragile flower that's uprooted, like. I know she's been sleeping badly the last six months. She doesn't speak or understand English. Sometimes she comes to see me here. She doesn't know about the rapes. I've told her I was dealing a bit of dope and in Canada the penalty's rough when they get you for it. Maria comes in, her eyes puffy. All the guys are watching her. My toes curl up in my shoes, I tear at the underside of the desk with my nails, and Maria sits down. Jack, the big guy who beat me up because I'd taken girls by force, can't resist asking her how come a beautiful woman like her puts up with a sonovabitch like me. She wants me to translate. I tell her all the prisoners think she's very beautiful and some of them aren't polite about it.

Maria, Maria. I pull the sheet up over my head and whisper the name, chew on it and breathe it out. Her hair's slowly growing back, she's lost some weight. Last week, her nails were painted blue. I imagine exciting situations which have no effect on my body any more. I lie on my stomach and see our apartment's bedroom, three-quarters filled with our very soft bed that's covered with several cozy, warm blankets. Maria's asleep beside me, wearing only a little pair of panties, her breasts bare. I hear her gentle breathing, I smell her girl's scent. If her hair was longer, I'd cover my face with it.

CHAPTER 6

Parker talked to me for an hour today at noon, after the group therapy session. I might be shut out of the group because I won't cooperate and talk about myself, and the things I've done, and my "sickness." I'd much rather stay in my cell and do nothing than listen to prisoners faking their therapy routines, and smell that slight sweat as the doctor gets excited in a vacuum. I don't want to be a circus animal. I'm not the one that's sick. It's Parker that needs to get off his butt and do something. At home at night, he must beat the meat like a wild man, fantasizing over the things he's been hearing all day. Out of jealousy or envy, he stuffs us full of pills that eventually keep us from seeing even the ends of our penises. Parker got to be a doctor for rapists because he wasn't brave enough to be a rapist himself. It was that or be a gynecologist, but the man probably can't get near a girl's crotch without falling apart. Calling us "sick" lets him feel righteous. He applies for grants, then takes in the most debauched and violent rapists in the country and, posing as a man of virtue who gives himself for the good of humanity, hypocritically neutralizes its most abject level while feeding the core of his fantasies from our sexual feats.

In the course of our talk, he told me I was "clever." I thought the word meant "spineless" or "dumb." It sounded empty, shapeless, and hollow, like the bodies of girls after rapes. When I've done a rape, I get away fast from the place so as not to be infected by the victim's distress. I like to read fear in those wide, misty eyes, the fear that comes after surprise, but I don't want to see what comes after that. That's why I blindfold a girl, gag her and tie her hands. It's not just so she can't recognize me at the police station, scream, or defend herself. No, there's something else. I wasn't as well equipped for my first rapes as I am now. I frightened the girls, and they let me do what I wanted. I would look in their eyes and try to read what was in them. When I'd finished my first rape, in Guatemala, I saw the forlorn look in my victim's eyes. She gave a stifled sob and curled up with her hands around her knees to protect herself from me, looking at me in a peculiar way. I wanted to comfort her and take her back home. In Montreal, I never let myself get emotionally involved. The only important thing has been my rage, what I've been doing, the way I'd make things go as I wanted. After a rape, I've been in a hurry to get away from the place, and the state the victim was in hasn't had time to get to me. To my great surprise, "clever" meant "intelligent." Parker admired me because I'd dared do what he was obsessed by. A feeble-minded old fool, if only he knew it.

I'm driven to do what I do by nature. My impulses come from the centre of the earth. In a given space, prey and predators move around nonchalantly. All have a feeling of what is ahead and are waiting for the equilibrium to be broken. The masculine forces meeting with the feminine. The prey knows that the serpent's fangs will one day sink into its sides, tear its tissues and open up its flesh. Like two pieces of a puzzle, a tooth, a rib, a tooth, a rib, meshed together as enamel and calcium grate in meeting. Then the serpent is freed of its aggressiveness and the prey is at peace. Worn out, the predator goes home as quiet as a lamb, while the animal bitten lies on its back, almost dead, revolted by the putrid stink of liquids caked on its skin, the blood, pus, plasma, sperm and saliva, its entrails exposed and swept by the breath of a foul wind. If Parker were a reptile, he'd be a cringing little grass snake, frightened by shrew mice, biting into wood, frustrated by the sight of a serpent and a doe hare in amorous embrace. Totally ignorant of the pleasure of emptying his anger into something truly living–a warm, moist body open there before him. Waiting for an emptying.

CHAPTER 7

I followed them one by one, without being seen, more or less. Ariane, my thirty-first, bumped my leg when walking in front of me and excused herself without even glancing at me. I narrowly avoided being hit full in the face by the strap on her backpack. We waited for the métro together, she reading a book, I ogling the back of her neck. On this first night of meeting, all I wanted was to know where she lived. She finally got off at the Pie IX Station. A guy came out of the next car and came to talk to her. So as not to lose face, I went and bought a big roll of tape–it could always come in handy–and the cheapest newspaper in the station convenience store. I sensed that they'd slept together. There was too little distance between their bodies and she had that way of squeezing his arm to reinforce what she was telling him whenever her voice rose. The guy's arms dangled and he seemed delighted by her touches.

A fine powder was falling, my very first snow. Never having set foot in this neighbourhood before, I memorized the names of streets that went by as I followed Ariane, fascinated by her light, airy step. We were wandering through the neighbourhood's labyrinth, the two of us. I could have eaten her alive in one of the lanes she knew so well. Appeared to her suddenly, cancelled all her reference points, tied her up with thread and loved her in a long, unending embrace.

I was an armed spy, an impatient animal preparing its attack and ready to explode like a bomb. Acid veins, effervescent arteries, a belly on fire, kamikazi lungs. Each breath threatened to set off an explosion that would shatter me into millions of little pieces. No one knew where I was at that moment. I crept and hid, my white weapon tight against my stomach. I trampled my tracks in the fresh snow to mess them up. Ariane's tracks were narrow, ending in a half-moon heel. I was my only master. Everything was going fine, the epilepsy was staying away.

The rape would take place the next day, a Tuesday like any other.

CHAPTER 8

Around the middle of October, when night catches up with day in Quebec, I followed a girl without intending to, without even noticing what I was doing. I was coming home from work and it was Friday. I'd got out of the bus behind her. I was thinking of anything but that girl; I was in a hurry to get home to the apartment, to kiss Maria and give her the bananas from Costa Rica that I had picked out for her one by one. I was even beginning to come round to the idea of having a baby with my wife. To make a long story short, I was a bit tired.

Ahead of me, the girl was hastening her steps. Her attitude was getting ridiculous, and that's what drew me out of my reverie. She was walking very fast, her noisy little heels tapping on the asphalt. Her enormously wide ass was squeezed into a pair of young professional's beige pants. Absorbed in my thoughts, I quickened my pace to match hers without really being aware of it. I suddenly had an urge to run after her or to come close and shout, "Boo!" That girl was terrified and her terror was exciting the anger in me. She sensed me behind, very close, or maybe my shadow was ahead of her. Maybe too she was frightened by the smell of me. I'd sweated a lot that day and I stank. I'd better take a shower before getting close enough to Maria to make love to her. The girl crossed the street, looking like one of those red cows you see on the roads in Central America.

All this intense paranoia marked her as a potential victim. Her whole being shouted, "Rape me somebody, let's get it over with, once and for all." Or maybe she'd been attacked before. Didn't matter. This girl was an invitation to rape, and a forecast of other attacks to come. She'd behaved like prey and wakened the predator in me.

I put my hand on her mouth and pushed her into a lane. I tore off her clothes without taking the trouble to undo the buttons. Her crotch became elastic in my hand. A cat watched us. I asked her what she was studying, so as to, I guess, personalize her rape a bit.

"Bio."

"What? I don't understand. Speak up you fat, ugly broad."

"Biology," she muttered.

I stuffed her gullet full of grass and earth. She spat and vomited on the cement when I penetrated her with one thrust. Two ants ran round on her back. We were alone and it was too easy. The backs of her thighs were marbled with varicose veins. Ugly. I bit her in the back till I made her bleed, so hard I had a bit of her flesh on the roof of my mouth. It tasted like the beef tongues my father used to make us eat. A tongue on a tongue, that's dumb! Raping a fat girl, am I ever dumb! I grabbed her mop of hair and pulled like I was ordering a horse to stop. That little face of a virtuous maiden imagining she was far, far away was driving me crazy. I ejaculated straight into the crack between her buns–that would teach her to go parading her fat ass in ridiculous pants like those. She didn't move, didn't say anything more, let me do what I wanted with her. I could have eaten every scrap of her piece by piece and she'd have let me do it, imagining she was somewhere else on a desert island with Brad Pitt. Dumb broad! I picked her up and threw her in a dumpster. I hadn't even needed to get out the adhesive tape. The knife in my pocket had stayed there all through the rape. It was really too easy. I don't advise anyone to rape an obese girl in an empty parking lot. It's as dull and insignificant as peeing down a drain on a rainy Sunday afternoon.

It was the prototype of an unplanned, inevitable rape, one that happens in a frenzy, that's unexpected, set off by something irrelevant. It was something that could happen now and then along a road of rapes. It was surely a sign of health.

Maria threw her arms around my neck. A smell of vegetables cooked with lemon was coming from the kitchen. She seemed half asleep; she must have spent the afternoon dozing in front of the TV, watching programs whose language she didn't understand. I told her a rapist was prowling round the neighbourhood and a girl who worked at the market had been assaulted.

"Now she's so scared she goes round holding keys in her hand so she can jab any man in the face who wants to have her."

Maria seemed to think that was awful. I took the beautiful yellow bananas out of my bag. Her look of horror turned to a smile. She began to laugh in that high-pitched voice of hers.

I would have liked her never to leave the apartment. She risked being attacked, and if it happened I would never have got over it. Girls who are too beautiful shouldn't expose themselves to everyone's sight; men see them and go crazy. I'd have given Maria anything to make her happy just to stay inside. I ordered her *rompope* from a Mexican grocery, I made *ceviche* and coconut custard every Saturday night, and every night I gave her hair a hundred strokes with a brush. I loved her. Yes, I loved Maria.

I always wondered what occupied her thoughts. I managed to keep her inside the apartment, but I would have liked to know what was going on inside of her. When I took the bananas out of their brown paper bag while I was talking about the raped girl, her face had flushed with joy in a matter of seconds. Did she feel threatened? Did she feel sympathy for that girl? Did she just not care about her? Or would she think about her as soon as I'd left? I would have liked to set up cameras in the apartment so as to see what Maria was doing while I was away, follow her through her moods, sleep as close as I could to her dreams, get myself into her memories and play a leading role in them, find out what slithered into her nights and made her grind her teeth while she slept.

CHAPTER 9

In grating concert, the doors of my cell glide to either side of the wall, allowing me to step into the corridor, which leads directly to the common room. At Penetanguishene Prison, this is recreation time for rapists and destroyers of childhood.

There in the big grey room, two abusers of little girls are playing billiards. Four others are at cards. I flop in an easy chair, helpless before an old Rubik's cube missing several coloured pieces. At three in the afternoon, of course, there's nothing interesting on the TV. I watch a women's program, thinking Maria would like it. Overaged Barbies and former top models who've seen better days are playing rich, genteel but pathetic ladies victimized by fops with toaster-sized jaws. So the lady sighs, has hysterics, discovers her mother is a swindler and she's lost every penny. I'm told I'm a fuckin' faggot, and I change channels.

Two children missing front teeth are making banana-ham-jujube-parsley sandwiches. I hear one of the pedophiles whisper to the other that it's even better when they don't have teeth. Disgusted, I click again. The pedophile yells and one of the rapists snaps at him:

"Mother-fucker, at least you could wait for their breasts to grow."

A guard comes out of his booth, adjusts the set to "Documentaries," and confiscates the remote control.

On the screen, a lion hides without being hidden behind lush, pale green bushes. A distant sound of trampling feet gradually turns into a rumbling, a reverberation rising from the ground that makes the tall grasses shake. The continuing sound approaches; now we can clearly make out the nervous, ungainly gallop of a herd of animals. With their slender legs and their yellow-brown coats and their heads crowned with spiralled horns, the gazelles are running, urgently. In their eyes shot through with awareness of danger, the lion reads fear and savours it, salivates as he watches a scene that awaits only his entry to assume its full significance. The gazelles slip across the field of vision of the predator, who is already gathering his rear limbs beneath his pale belly, lowering his head, and trembling, eyes alert. At last he leaps and breaks the flowing rhythm of a herd of prey in flight. The animals slow to a trot, massed head to tail, then speed up again in two fast streams, one either side of the lion. They know. He makes them wait, closes his eyes, and in a flash seizes one by a thigh. The gazelle crashes to the ground, forcing those following to avoid it by all manner of acrobatics. It could have been another. This one was neither sick nor weaker than others. Its eyelids heavy, an average gazelle lies on the ground waiting for its flesh to be torn apart like a grocery bag.

CHAPTER 10

When my Uncle Tío showed me how to read, I'd just turned eight years old. He'd told my father to let up on me with the cows and send me to school. They'd fought and rolled in a heap of manure. They'd begun to laugh, and from that day on, I spent my mornings reading and my afternoons milking. We read *Cien años de soledad* for a couple of years. There were about thirty stories in a single story. My uncle would bring coffee and I would dissolve sugar in it. We'd soak pieces of dry bread in the steaming coffee and I would be elated by the ritual. While I read, my mother attended to the baby and my father sweated like a pig in the barn.

Coffee, books, insomnia and a stiff cock pointing at the sky: all that came into my life at the same time. My nights were criss-crossed by women with round butts, by wild girls straight out of the forest with their hair full of insects, crazy eyes that frightened me and triangular breasts giving the sky the come-on, just like my prick.

You'd have thought my uncle had all the world's stories inside of him. We read, yes, but he told me some fascinating stories from his own life too. I'd thought for years that he was really a writer whose dead right arm, wounded by an exploding shell, prevented him from holding a pencil. He told me about war. I learned to read and about politics. I wasn't sleeping any more because I'd so much rather think about all these new things dancing around inside my skull.

Still today, as soon as they lock me in my cell, I lie down on the cot with my arm under my head, and it all starts galloping in there. My thoughts return to Ariane, then Maria, Anna, Nurse Smith and the others, girls I've raped. I'm a child, an infant, at that! I'm wrapped in blankets and laid in a cradle made of bamboo and am surrounded by girls oo-ing and ahh-ing over me. I whimper a bit, get Nurse Smith's flabby nipple full in the mouth and drink from it. Generous bosoms watch over me, see to my well-being, busy themselves around the cradle, languorous breasts following the movements of the girls, a half-beat behind. One girl diapers me, another cooks, I'm cajoled, taken to the river, always snuggled against generous torsos. We're in the very middle of a peaceful clearing. Aromas of tomatoes, pepper and meat are escaping from a large pot. Around us, gazelles and antelopes graze as they wait in resignation for a devouring. I, a mis-shapen child-animal, will orchestrate the carnage. Mauve muscles will snap and die between my teeth. I will gorge on vitamin-rich organs still quivering from being not quite dead. When I am full, I will mount open, worthless haunches, luxurious with never-healing wounds. They'll have been waiting for this ultimate moment of fertilization since I was born. From these girls' flesh, opened by the force of nature, other Minotaurs will spring. The empty bellies of killed gazelles will fly away in the talons of violent birds. The gazelles' light bones will roll where the wind will carry them to enrich the grass and life below ground, which is already fed by their bloodless bodies.

A rattle of keys in the lock rouses me from my dream.

"Torrès, Mino, come here."

CHAPTER 11

I don't know where I am any more. I wake sometimes convinced that Maria's asleep beside me. I whisper in Spanish. Always when I wake up and hear the barred doors opening to let the first prisoners out into the corridor, I think I'm in Guatemala near the Inter-Americana and big trucks are making our house shake. My mother making coffee, Anna putting on makeup in the bathroom, the radio crackling, little spiders on the ceiling, and a lizard running all the way down the wall. Again it's Spanish that comes to my lips. Then I realize that, no, I have to speak another language, and I switch to French and at last I'm completely awake, I see my cell and I hear the guys talking in English. Reality hits me like a fly crashing suddenly into my eye.

It seems they're going to send me back to where I came from after my sixteen years in prison. It's nearly six months I've been here inside these high, dreary walls. I feel like I'm in a place that's out of place, in a non-country, and I'm speaking a borrowed, all-purpose language. I've even forgotten the name of the detention centre I'm in, a word that sounds like a prisoner vomiting his guts.

I decided to immigrate to Montreal because they speak French there and my uncle had taught me the language. As soon as we'd finished reading *Cien años de solidad,* we started it again, but in French this time. I was convinced that this was the only book in the world, written in a thousand languages, so you could read it an infinite number of times since, in any event, you would have forgotten the beginning which you'd read two years earlier. From then on my uncle had me read only in French. We even ended up reading poems filled with women who were lesbians and magical. Quebec wasn't as far away as France, anyway, in case I wanted to come back. I'd read somewhere that Montreal was a cosmopolitan city, and I said to myself, Well, Maria can make some Latino girlfriends there.

Raping had become too easy in Guatemala. I was a middling good rapist now and I wanted a bit more challenge. I'd heard that the girls in Canada had a lot of freedom, went to university and into politics, wrote books, did things just like men do. I wanted to debase a white girl who was liberated, unsubmissive, intellectual, and beautiful. I'd give her what was coming to her and she'd see first hand what nature has ordained.

In prison, there are only two possible activities: watching TV or dreaming. My dreams are the only things that really belong to me. There are dreams awake, that we force a bit, and the others, the ones when we're asleep, that are innate in sleep. Those are the most exciting ones. We fall crazily into bottomless pits, the people around us are interchangeable, we're as light as bubbles. In dreams, awake or asleep, we're always the central point, the pivot around which events unfold. Everything happens through us. Inside ourselves, we possess the way things go and we can choose to end them when we want.

The guards don't like it when the prisoners dream. Every time I do it, sooner or later I hear keys in the lock of my cell and a big bruiser comes in and for no good reason shakes me out of it.

I'd like to rape a mute girl. She'd be strong and would fight me. But she wouldn't have even a tiny voice. Before fear appeared in her eyes, she'd show me her martial arts techniques without a word. I have a horror of female voices. They drive me crazy. The higher pitched they are, the harder I could twist an arm. For me, every woman who talks is a torture. She might almost get away, but I'd be sure to end up pulling out my knife, and then she'd finally be afraid and spread her legs. I'd make her come and she'd find her voice again so I'd stab her. That's the way it is.

It's rising in me, I can feel it. I give it a few more minutes to break. I tremble, my tongue thickens, my mouth is dry. I pant a bit, it's holding off though my body's getting warm. It's like a tide that starts in the middle of the ocean and keeps coming and then breaks on all sides. My lungs contract and my ribs separate, my buttocks tighten, my body's a battleground, a minefield. At last the seizure comes!

CHAPTER 12

A Blockbuster membership, a coupon for a free Second Cup coffee, a movie ticket, business cards from Hamel's cheese shop and a Greek bakery on St. Laurent Boulevard, a Mexican restaurant menu folded twice, a few tokens for playing video games at the Crystal Palace, a packet of hashish, 20 dollars, a bill for a coat, a Bell telephone bill, and a third year high school student identity card of Ariane's, with her little imp, laughing hussy look. Three policemen spread all there was in my wallet on the kitchen table, each item like one more proof of my guilt. The room filled gradually with a smell of poached sole.

When I saw the three police cars through the window, I realized it was at the apartment of one of the girls I'd love-raped that I'd dropped my wallet. I ordered Maria to go into our bedroom, telling her reassuringly that I'd had my wallet stolen at work, that the policemen thought they'd found out who the kleptomaniac was but they were carrying out a preliminary investigation.

I was almost relieved when they arrested me. I think I would have kept on raping at a crazy rate. The victims calmed me, I ran to them frantically, they haunted me then abandoned me, so I had to begin again every time, like in a play endlessly rehearsed, that stimulates with improvement, with the fine-tuning of details I'd been missing at first, the ease I'd acquired in my movements, the flow of sequences, the growing assurance, the bitter pleasure of giving the gift of fear.

I felt the leaden metal of the handcuffs clamp around my wrists.

"You know how they work, don't you?" the fat investigator snarled in my ear. I'd fastened my last two victims' ankles together with handcuffs (too big for the fragile hands they'd meekly offered). I longed to go to sleep and was feeling somewhat the effect of the blows I'd taken to my body, the vice-like grip of a hand squeezing my jaw, the rubber bounce of a nightstick on my lax muscles.

Maria was screaming and weeping. They took me away in a car as neighbours who'd come out on their balconies for the occasion looked on, intrigued. A smell of burnt fish followed me as I went, with my wife throwing onions at the policemen and yelling an appallingly vulgar Guatemalan slang which was lost in the dry air of a merciless November.

I was as oblivious to the scene as to one of a beautiful blind girl trying to find her reflexion in a mirror. I would never rape a blind girl. You can see all kinds of things in the eyes of the girls you take. It happens in three phases. First there's surprise. The girl isn't really worried. Ariane even laughed! (But Ariane is Ariane.) The best is to come. You have to watch for it because the moment is so brief, like the green ray of light at the end of a sunset. Then you can see raw fear in their eyes, terror, panic. From that moment on, it's as if they've already accepted that they're going to be raped. You control them totally; they surrender. No resistence is offered, you can do what you want with them. Here again, with Ariane it didn't go that way. With her, I was feeling shame. I was looking dumb because she wasn't afraid. She wasn't playing her role of prey, didn't seem to understand what was happening. That's why I beat her up so much. She had to know I was dangerous. In the third phase–I dread this one–their eyes fill with all the world's sadness and suffering. I blindfold the girls so as not to have to take in that vision of horror, which kills me. Otherwise, what I see in those eyes reminds me too much of Maria begging me to make her a baby. Anyway, after ejaculating I wait three seconds and then take off.

CHAPTER 13

My hollow cough sounded like the bleat of a lonely animal calling in vain to its kind. Or the lament of a mammal digesting its young after swallowing them to protect them from a predator. For the first time in my life I had a winter cold. And my trial was under way.

From my bronchial tubes, salty secretions waltzed up to my throat and all the way to my tongue. I stared at a glass on the desk; it had been empty for a while already. Sensing the rise of a more phlegmy coughing spell, I had drunk the lawyer's water. I wasn't paying much attention to her argument; I was pleading guilty to three rapes and two attempted murders. Things were going to end up badly anyway.

The third victim was there and was looking at me hard, pleased with herself for having spat in my face with her family there to back her up. While being accused, I was being called *"Monsieur"* and was spoken to politely. I'd rather have police brutality than judicial hypocrisy. Each time I heard my name I'd stop coughing, rouse from my torpor, look at the audience, and meet the angry gaze of the girl at whose apartment I'd dropped my wallet. She wasn't testifying; she was there and she kept staring at me.

I was feeling uncomfortable. Not because of what I'd done, no, but because of that look she kept throwing at me, which pierced me like a sharp, pointed object. Her eyes were now emptied of fear; she was no longer offered to me without the least defence. Her family and the stabbed lover were behind her. Their eyes were echoing the same mix, in diluted strength, of hate and contempt. To them, I was evil incarnate.

I kept hoping to see Ariane arrive. Hoping she'd turn up in court for a spell and see me properly, without tape over her eyes. Only her house-mate was there and I amused myself by staring at him. He couldn't stand it and looked away.

Ariane understood why I did what I did. Maybe she even had a little compassion for me. There was a big clothes closet in her bedroom. I hid in it, sitting on two cardboard boxes, wary of skis that were threatening to fall down on me. On the shelves, little coloured bottles, perfume samples, books and magazines were heaped this way and that in a real girl's muddle. And broken cassettes, frayed scarves, ski boots, laundry detergent, a wig, a dusty old computer, an empty port bottle, and a partly open chocolate box holding coloured pencils. The legs of a clown costume dangled onto my shoulders. A pink costume with white dots. I hoped I'd find the courage I'd need to jump on Ariane. I had to. Otherwise, I would have come out of the closet when she'd gone to the kitchen or the bathroom and I'd have got out of there. Her cat came and sniffed at me. She came into view. And the rest is known.

We had a pause around 10:15 and the lawyer bought me some cough drops and told me things were going pretty badly for me, that I'd probably get 15 years at the very least. That day I didn't give much of a shit. Aching from head to toe, exhausted from a night spent coughing, I was delighted by the prospect of a permanently assured bed, of not having to answer to anyone, and of not having to go to work. Constant rest was the right solution to the accumulation of fatigue I was feeling in all the joints of my body.

If I could have died on the spot, I would have done it.

CHAPTER 14

Yellow intermittent lines pierced the autoroute. I counted them quickly, imagining my mother's needle basting a pants-leg hem. Everything was going by very fast. Next I was staring at the street lamps also going by very fast. Now and then a sign punctured the sky, screaming unfamiliar directions. I drowsed the way one rapes, filled with rage. The car's engine lulled me incompletely. I would have liked that moment to last forever, then I'd have passed out not knowing if I was going to sleep or dying, just like in my epileptic seizures.

Ariane was like a fish I might have pulled out of the water. She was prettier than the teenager on the student cards. Ariane is the opposite of Maria. Ariane is life; Maria is death. With Maria, the best is sleeping. She massages your back and sometimes sucks you to wake you up. If I could only spend a night with Ariane, I'd inject something in my veins and have a sleepless night in a fantastic delirium of virility. I nearly killed Ariane with my hands, though she was the one who most deserved to live. Among the books in her apartment, there were two by Gabriel Garcia Marquez, *One Hundred Years of Solitude,* but also *Chronicle of a Death Foretold.* I had come to Montreal to rape Ariane. She was that beautiful, educated Blanche who wouldn't give in without a fight. Instead of spreading her legs and offering herself to me so I could take her, control her, command the scene from beginning to end, she didn't understand what I was there for. She tried to get away, bashed at me with what energy she had left. I never expected things might go that way. With her like that, I couldn't have got it up any more than I could in front of these two policemen escorting me. Ariane, Ariane,

Ariane. Her name echoes in my head, hovers between my temples. I respect her and know she's thinking of me at this moment.

The two policemen throw victorious glances at me. I can well imagine how humdrum their daily lives must be. To them, I'm the bad guy they've captured and put in a cage. They're proud of it and will go home and tell the little wifey the whole story so she'll get all weak-kneed over her man's virility. And they'll secrete babies to convince themselves of their love.

As for me, I did my thing. I had a moment of control over my life, over Ariane's, and the lives of a lot of other girls who came my way at the right time.

"A bowl-shaped receptacle closely perforated at the bottom and used for draining liquids." That's a colander. I learned the word at work at the Jean-Talon Market.

"Potatoes gotta be washed. Use a colander," said Pierre, another seller at the market.

I went and looked it up in the dictionary that evening when I went home. Maybe Pierre has raped a girl, I said to myself. The bread delivery girl in her big truck, lying on those plump round loaves and warm baguettes. Or perhaps the girl who often bought our strawberries, smiling. In the end, there wasn't much difference between girls and colanders.

CHAPTER 15

"Our society has painted man as a dynamic warrior and woman as a passive consoler and care-giver. This view of things must change; these traditional roles should no longer be held as models. We should recognize the equality of the sexes." Dr. Parker rambles on like this.

I hate to be preached at. Parker is a conquistador; he's trying to convert us, walk all over us, and evangelize us, instil the common sense of his morality in us. The only rule I obey is to have no rules. If I hadn't choked Ariane I would have died of shame. She was controlling the game. Her eyes showed amusement, puzzlement, all kinds of strange things. She was perhaps too accustomed to people being nice. But I was violent, armed, someone to be afraid of. To survive me, she'd have to understand she wasn't dealing with some clown.

I won't tell Parker why I rape. "I'm not going to do your work for you," I told him.

That won't do me much good, I guess. I didn't know what rape was before reading *Cronica de una muerta anunciata* by Garcia Marquez. I didn't understand what was going on. My uncle was surprised and we began to talk about girls. I'd been with Maria for several years and we rarely made love.

"Raping is taking someone by force," Tío explained, shifting his pelvis.

"Oh, okay! So I was raped by *putas* on a volcano."

Tío laughed hard and told me how, in wars he'd conducted as regimental sergeant-major, there were women in droves. He and his men would march over soils that were dried out and strewn with still bodies. Sometimes they would find a skinny woman with a child in an old hut. What a bellyful that woman had of it! The whole gang came a-visiting. There was nothing left of those two by the time they'd all trooped through.

From that point on, my uncle undertook to make a man of me. He lent me his truck, signifying, Go get yourself a woman. When they give me back my freedom, I'm still going to want to pump my rage into girls' bodies, more than ever, probably. There'll be a lot of attacks, because all this bitterness and boredom I'm full of already only grow in prison and they'll have to be got out of me.

This afternoon on the *Documentaries* channel, they showed a program on the major volcanos of Central America. I was thirteen the first time I got inside a girl. It was near the Arenal volcano in Costa Rica. My friend Manuel's father was going to Costa Rica to bring back a truckload of sheep and Manuel and I went along. Manuel's father left us with his sister and was to come back and get us a few days later. Eduardo, the twenty-year-old cousin, had just bought a car and wanted to take us to spend the night in San José. The place was in a party mood because of elections coming up. People were dressed in green and white, or red and blue, depending on their political allegiances. Eduardo bought us a bottle of cane alcohol, and we were drinking in a park waiting for him to come back from a discothèque. I was so dazzled by what was going on around me, I was knocking back the *cacique*. The ground was littered with streamers, garlands, and red, white, green, and blue confetti. Three men were fighting without being really serious about it. The children who had begged cigarettes from us had retreated under a bench with their noses in a glue bag. On a soiled political poster of one of the candidates, two dogs were fornicating; the male, of rather diminutive size, was going at it as if his life depended on it, stuffing a fat bitch who didn't seem to realize she was being mounted.

"Would you like a stuffed pomelo?"

Maria and her younger sister Lorenita were selling fruit and flowers.

"You cut the pomelo in two and you find treats inside: syrup, candied fruit, a little honey, crunchy things. My mother made them and everybody wonders how she empties them and then fills them without leaving marks you can see. It's a secret. Take a look. If you find how, I'll give it to you."

I poured a little alcohol into a party cone-hat for Maria. We ate a pomelo. Her sister went to join the children under the bench. I didn't know where Manuel had gone and didn't give much of a damn. To put it short, I was getting drunk. I kissed Maria on the neck and we went together under a tree. We rolled together in the confetti as if it was snow. Eduardo arrived blowing his horn, like a lunatic. There seemed to be five people in the car.

"Mino, come, and I swear you'll have the best night of your life," Eduardo pronounced with an enigmatic smile. Manuel was already on board. I wanted to bring Maria and Lorenita, but Eduardo made a face as though displeased. "Where d'you think we'll put them? On the roof?" I asked him to give me two minutes.

Maria put the pomelo tray back in place, passing the strap around her neck and losing the end in her abundance of hair.

"I'll do all I can to come back to this park tomorrow afternoon," I promised her.

I left her the bottle of alcohol, asking her to drink a little toast to my health. She laughed and her pink tongue and scent of citrus fruits delighted me. Her sister arrived, smelling of glue, and then I joined Eduardo and Manuel in the car, thinking that the only thing I didn't like about Maria was her size. Standing, she was a little taller than me.

On the back seat, Manuel and I were squeezed between two women. They were very warm friends, Eduardo and his friend Leandro said. I asked Leandro if they were friends of his mother's or what, because I didn't know them. He shoved a cigarillo in my mouth and told me that in thirty minutes these women would be my best friends and I wouldn't want to be separated from them after that. I had an ample bosom on my shoulder and it reeked of perfume. Someone was playing in my hair, and I imagined it was Maria.

We were driving toward the Arenal. Leandro was studying natural sciences and was working in that field. The volcano was sometimes dangerous but not just then. Incandescent lava-flows were trickling down the north side, which was to be avoided, but we were headed for the south flank. In a violent thrust, the monster belched red-hot stones and jets of fire. As we ascended, the trees shrank and their leaves were growing as broad as umbrellas. Elated, Eduardo bellowed how beautiful life was.

"Manuelito, Minolito, this is the most beautiful day of your lives!" he said as he stopped the vehicle with the radio left playing.

Eduardo and Leandro danced with the women. We watched and did the same thing, awkwardly. The women were taller than us. I would have liked to experience all this with Maria. Conchita had a beard and little moustache of dark, downy hair. Her eyebrows touched, it was ugly. All her flesh was flabby and her big, fleshy mouth frightened me. Her dangling tongue, her thighs, her flapping calf muscles, and her breasts that were bigger than her head–Conchita's body was like a labyrinth I had no wish to get lost in. I wanted a citrus-flavoured cat's tongue, pointed teeth, lively eyes, a slightly torn dress. No moustache or hairs. Behind us, the volcano was going crazy. What there was under Conchita's skirt was like a dead animal, a disembowelled groundhog.

Leandro rolled in the grass with Conchita while Eduardo let his penis be licked by Victoria on the roof of his car. Maria was in my head, pursuing me, I felt she could see me, and I watched the Arenal instead of the women because I was ashamed. What I was doing was dirty. I wanted to leave, but I was caught in a trap on this volcano. A phrase kept coming back to my mind, like a line of a song: "Would you like a stuffed pomelo?" My fruit seller had a beauty spot just under her eye.

The women spread their legs. Eduardo and Leandro had bet on Manuel and me. We took our places at the start of the race. It was the Leandro-Mino team mounted on Conchita against Eduardo-Manuel and their mare Victoria. I didn't want to be there. Manuel reached the finish line in less than a minute. As for me, I had the impression I was getting swallowed up in an open wound, falling into a sea of warm flesh. I looked at the volcano, Conchita's enormous breasts, the phosphorescent bubblings leaping from the mouth of the Arenal, I heard Leandro's bellows and moans from Conchita, and did everything possible not to see her eyes.

All my muscles were stiff. My movements seemed to me ridiculous, repetitive, deserving anger. I felt this was not exactly the way one had to go about it. That I was behaving like a lizard, wriggling the middle of my body like a twisted see-saw. Conchita was like a stricken animal expelling her last puffs of air. That down at her throat, which she was offering me shamelessly. Her eyes that were turned up, frighteningly. And Maria who must still be selling candied fruit in an unkempt park. I thought of these things to forget my penis swallowed up in Conchita's belly. It seemed to me I'd reached a point of no return. I kept going and was getting nowhere. I thought of other things to anaesthetize these feelings. It was too private to be spread out in plain view for Leandro, Eduardo, Manuel, and Victoria, who was putting her skirt back on close by. My whole body was swollen, rivers of blood were coursing through my veins in great floods to irrigate my penis. I felt the scene was going to go on for ever.

I was going to be sick.

I withdrew suddenly, crushing Conchita's little finger, and threw up in a bush. Curtly, Eduardo and Leandro herded us all into the car. No one said a word during the return drive. Eduardo spat through the window at regular intervals. Leandro turned up the radio volume. The smell of the women made my stomach heave. They got out in downtown San José. When he paid them, Eduardo apologized, saying he'd thought we were men but in the end we were still only children. Victoria was fixing her hair as they talked and Conchita was repainting her lips red. We passed the place where I'd met Maria.

The park was deserted and shabby, like Conchita's crotch. A dog was sniffing at a garbage can. If I had not been so drunk, I would have been enraged. For a long time the sugar cane fields marched by on either side of the road in silence.

I woke the next day in mid-morning with an impression of having dreamed a lot, a feeling of shame doubly fed by memories of Maria and Eduardo, and a burning penis. An uproar was coming from the kitchen: the grandmother had died in her sleep.

"Go and wake him up," cried Manuel's aunt, in tears.

Eduardo burst into the room where we were sleeping and flung open the curtains. "Roll this round your prick and get up. Abuela's dead."

Manuel winced as he grabbed the roll of gauze and then left the room. An hour later, the house had emptied.

I had my breakfast watching the TV in the living room beside the old woman's body, which was lying in state on the buffet. I'd prepared a dish of fruit to clean my mouth in anticipation of my meeting with Maria. I chewed at length on juicy little lemons, I covered my gums with melon slices, and I rubbed my teeth with orange peels. My penis was throbbing with pain, so I let it hang in a glass of hot water, hoping that the pain would pass.

I took my shower and rubbed the glans, howling with pain; hard white pustules were poking through my already raw-rubbed flesh. I wrapped my penis in the gauze that Manuel had forgotten beside Abuela's bathtub, put on clean clothes, then, avoiding the feet of the dead woman which were protruding beyond the end of the buffet, left the house.

I went by bus. I had to wait an hour for Maria. The park had been cleaned and the previous evening returned to my head in curious gusts. Now I knew what a girl was. She could be a mixture of candied fruits, pointed teeth, fragile caresses, shy kisses and a little sister high on drugs; or else a big flabby crotch with a hole, invasive perfume, noisy earrings, lipstick on Eduardo's penis, legs spread and saying nothing as she gives you mini-volcanos that itch. A woman was now someone I could form an opinion about: she was either pretty and fragile or she was venal and cynical.

The moist nose of a dog woke me, followed by Maria's crystalline laugh. From that day on she has never left me, except when I'm working or raping. Manuel's uncle came back from the South of the country to attend the funeral, and we stayed in Costa Rica for two weeks. I was with Maria all the time; Manuel and his family seemed too traumatized by Abuela's death to worry about my not being around. The eruptions of boils on my penis stopped after ten days. Maria came back with me to Guatemala and we were married when we were seventeen.

CHAPTER 16

They've segregated the prison's seven real scumbags. We didn't commit our crimes for a reason, and that makes us monsters, animals, beyond understanding. Jack, the big guy who's boss of Three Wing, has killed eight people over drugs and settlements of accounts, which in the eyes of the others makes him a less cruel, more reasonable, and less dangerous person than me.

My neighbour assaulted a girl he'd taken home with him after the bars had closed. He spends his time during therapy sessions muttering the same questions: "Why'd she come to my place? Why'd she lie down on my bed if she didn't want any of that?" Sometimes he repeats these questions even in his sleep. The other rapist is an influential man, an artists' manager. He's abused his power more than once to force a girl to fuck with him. He's older and looks down on the rest of us. He'll get out before long, thanks to his contacts.

One of the pedophiles has molested dozens of children. An Englishman, from England, who looks permanently dazed. He's scrawny and his oval face seems to have come from someone else's body. The more I think about it, the more I'd say he has a child's head, a clown's, a fat-cheeked baby's with a mongolian's eyes. He never talks and you'd swear he's just waking up from a deep coma. He eats two boiled eggs every morning.

Physically, there's nothing special about the three others. One ran a daycare before the scandal broke, another is a shoe salesman, and the third is a university professor. They're unfriendly and boring.

In the common room it's always the same: the impresario reads magazines in a corner; these three and the other rapist play cards or billiards; Egg-pate–the Englishman–does crossword puzzles, and I watch TV. When the remote control hasn't been confiscated and the guard seems absorbed in his paperwork, I deliberately pick a children's program; God knows in the afternoon there are plenty of *niños* in the parks and daycares. Children being taught to lace up their espadrilles, crunched up on the floor, doing their damndest to count their toes, and mothers putting hats or bulky wool tuques on their heads. Yellow buses coming to pick them up. In the children's programs, adults look either like feeble-minded retards or perverts who'd go as far as dipping their penises in a bucket of Smarties to entice toothless little mouths to play with them. Now and then I see the four pedophiles turn briefly toward the screen. And I'd like us to be caught on film so Dr. Parker could see how his chickenshit therapies have failed.

CHAPTER 17

At ten years old, I killed my father. I've never told anyone, but now that I'm in prison.... I told the story today during therapy. If I integrate well with the group, Parker has promised to stop my anti-erection pills, so I invent all kinds of stories. This one is special in that it's true, even though it's the least likely of any of them. Once I can get it up again, I'll be able to do something other than watch TV or dream. At least, then my dreams will lead somewhere; they'll bring on a feeling.

So my father died when I was ten. He used to drive big trucks full of cows all over the country, like Manuel's father. One morning he told me to come with him.

"I'll come if you let me hold the wheel on the highway," I told him.

It was a queer kind of day. Bolts of lightning streaked across the sky like shooting stars. The truck drove along at top speed over a flawless road surface that was so smooth you'd think you were on a moving sidewalk. Beside the highway, an old woman was selling pancakes at a little stand. Her face was like a dried-up old apple. She poured a kind of pale molasses over everything and her hair trailed in the pancake batter. The calves mooed now and then and as I ate my meal I avoided looking at their gentle eyes.

My father picked his teeth and I badgered him to drive. He pointed out the caymans in the streams bordering the highway to distract me. Raindrops were whipping the windscreen.

"You'll drive later. It's raining now and it's slippery."

I dropped off to sleep, lulled by the regular beating of raindrops and numbed by the smell of calves' urine; I woke in mid afternoon with a door handle imprinted on my cheek. We were arriving at the auction.

We passed empty trucks coming in the opposite direction as well as others full of magnificent cattle or animals headed for slaughter. There were two kinds of buyers here: breeders and butchers. The breeders showed their interest by holding up small sticks of green plastic and the butchers signalled their offers with red cards. Before the arrival of the bovines, we watched the horse show. The horses came from Central America for the most part, except for a few Andalusian stallions and sturdy Dutch mares imported to add backbone to indigenous breeds. My father adored horses. Cattle were beginning to bore him, so a few years earlier he had launched into raising Paso Fino horses. He owned a stallion, three breeder mares and four colts. My father wanted to make us nothing less than the best Paso Fino breeders in Central America.

The horses had been showered, rubbed down, and groomed, and their splendid legs contrasted with the abraded hocks of our calves. They travelled with padded bandages rolled from their hoofs to their flanks. An American would announce the breed of the horses which would then enter the ring, behaving skittishly. A dappled Andalusian with black-painted hoofs and ears well pricked, their tips feathery along the inside edge, made his entrance with parade step, sporting a penis a metre long that looked like a fifth leg, led by a Spanish woman in a scarlet dress. The buyers redoubled their oohs, whistles came from the four corners of the ring, my father stopped sucking on his toothpick, and I asked him if he was looking at the Andalusian's dead leg or the woman's frou-frous. He gave me a little cuff on the back of my head and told me I could drink the dregs of his beer if I liked. The stallion pivoted a half-turn on his back legs; I saw his flanks heaving very fast and his nostrils cover with frothy foam. The Spanish woman passed in front of us; she was so heavily made up I wondered if she wasn't a transvestite. The horse's knees were rising almost into the small of his mistress's back, he was bolting, but she controlled him with a firm hand and a sexual smile that showed her gums.

After the sale of the stallion, the seats around the ring emptied. Outside, bright-coloured blankets were slipped over the horses' backs, their legs were wrapped again from fetlocks to hocks, and they were led into other vehicles, those of their new owners. Then the second auction began, the more abject, the one about food, animals parading like cuts of meat, potential steaks and chops. There were fewer buyers around the ring, mostly men with red cards. Only the price of a dark bull with powerful horns was contested among the breeders. My father drove his truck in close to the entrance to the ring and let the calves out into the corridor; they were weak from the long, jostling ride on the highway and plodded along, their flanks scratched and scraped, too weary to resist.

Outside it was already dark. The horses were munching on rotting hay, and the cows were eating oats that were already germinating. I climbed onto the roof of a transport truck to see what was going on. My father seemed relieved to have sold his calves, all of them suffering from some strange illness. He had been very much afraid the illness would affect our horses and was counting on getting rid of the cattle at the first opportunity. First our goat had died, then the calves had been contaminated, and he had to act before the Paso Fino family was decimated. He was talking to a man who was pouring strong alcohol into cups then siphoning it into his mouth, which was toothless, crowned with abscesses and dried up like an old sponge. The man was holding an old yellow cow on a tether, letting it graze not far away. Apparently he wanted to sell it. But my father had told me privately that before buying any more cattle we'd have to clean out the barn and the truck with lime and hot water and let them air for a week so as to drive out the illness the calves had been sickening for.

The Spanish woman passed in front of me again, hellbent astride a big horse at the gallop, followed by a skinny fellow whipping a pony that was leaping ahead as fast as it could. She jumped the fence separating the auction site from the fields of corn and was disappearing at top speed when she changed her mind and suddenly pivoted her mount to see where her companion had got to. Without the make-up, she looked more like a woman. She had traded her temptress smile for a mocking grin and her bullring red dress for a riding costume–close-fitting mouse-grey trousers, a dark jacket that accentuated her slim waist and curvaceous hips, and long, black leather boots. But most important was her chignon undone and her abundant hair falling to the small of her back.

The pony refused point blank to jump the fence, stopping before the obstacle despite the whippings and roughness of his shamed rider. The woman was laughing herself breathless, taunting the man for being a loser and raking him and his nag with scorn. She asked him if he still wanted to offer himself to her, yes or no. If yes, he would have to jump the fence without delay because she was close to being tired of the ridiculous situation. Her laugh made our eardrums ring and–in her Spanish accent that was as round as her hips–she drove him to distraction by calling him a clown who wouldn't even be hired by a third-rate circus. The guy took it out on the nag, raining blows on it. The woman ordered him to let it be, swearing that in less than five minutes, even with a pony, she could jump that silly little obstacle. She said she only hung out with excellent riders and he had unfortunately not passed the test, putting him in his place as a schoolmarm would. The man, already in a deep pit of shame, replied in a choked voice that the *señorita* could ride that rigged course alone because, in any case, the *señorita* seemed to think that no one was as good as she was and he had had enough of her misplaced conceit. But she was already galloping away and her horse was kicking up its heels, sending mud flying and demeaning him even more. Her aristocratic profile could no longer be seen, only her hair flying above the ears of corn, though bursts of her laughter could still be heard, dramatic, withering, like a thousand little monsters of arrogance.

That girl deserved to die.

My father was looking for me because we had to leave as soon as possible. My mother had asked that we be back that same night. I could have hidden or stayed on the top of the truck a while longer without him finding me. I really wanted to see the Spanish woman come back, but since my father seemed tired and unsteady, I climbed down right away. He smelled of sugar, alcohol, and sweat. He'd sweated so much the armpits of his shirt had turned from blue to green. I knew that vinegary smell he carted round from morning to night, specially when he was working in the stable. Sometimes I felt like whomping him with a shovel, he stank so bad. It would grab me, like that, then I'd be ashamed of having thought of such a thing and I'd understand that a man who's a prisoner of a smell like that is more to be pitied than beaten.

He'd drunk rum or *cacique* and had knocked back a big black coffee to counteract the effect of the joy drinks. We climbed into the truck, whose empty box swung at the slightest curve.

My father was dead drunk.

On the highway, he talked about women, then about my mother; he said how much better it was to keep from mixing women and animals, 'cause you saw how she was, that Spanish girl, that witch. Ah! I noticed she didn't leave you cold, but you got to avoid girls like that like the plague or they'll do you in, my little Mino.

"*Papá,* I'd like to hold the wheel now," I told him, because anyway he was having trouble driving in a straight line. If I held the wheel and he took care of the pedals, maybe it would be better already, at least we'd avoid hitting the few vehicles coming the other way at this late hour.

Twenty minutes later I killed my father. I was concentrating on the yellow intermittent line. I was imagining an infinite pants-leg hem basted in yellow thread. The vision was numbing me, so I counted lamp standards for a change instead. I was sleepy. My father was still muttering. He talked about women's hips, backs, legs, as if he was taking one of them apart in front of me. He opened the window to spit and I asked him to leave it open. My eyes became dry and I fell asleep.

Things are fuzzy at that point. When I woke I made a wrong move: a 90-degree turn to the right. I was abruptly thrown out the left window while my father landed in the ditch, pierced through by the shattered windshield, crushed by the truck still contaminated by a curious illness.

My father died drunk.

I said, "Get out of there, you stinking old souse."

I called him all the names I could think of: drunkard, old rag, prickhead, rot pile, three-legged dog, foul breath, calf with an imaginary illness, bucket of lime, punctured lung, stable rat, road apple with rum, lousy rider, dead fish, pink vomit puddle, house garbage, woman, meat, steak, blood, all-the-world's-bad-smells-in-one-room, head like a fly-brained pony's hoof.

"Wake up! *Mamá*'s going to be worried. She won't sleep all night. You want her to imagine something serious has happened, eh? You want her to suspect the worst of the worst? Maybe she'll think we've had an accident. Get up, you old rubbish, crazy man's trash can, stream of piss, outcast. You want to get eaten by caymans, that it? You're really dumb, 'cause caymans have got pointed teeth, like mouse bones, and they're sharp like knives. So hurry up or you'll have a reptile smile sunk in your leg, and it seems that mark can stay. For life. Come on now, get up, you ugly old thing."

I hollered like this in the direction of the ditch till daylight sent its first faint rays into the coolness of the night, like the sun's lazy emissaries. I kicked at all the drops of dew clinging like pearls along the blades of grass. There were cries of birds and monkeys. An armadillo not far from me munched on flowers that were barely open, it was so early. The mauve sky made me feel nauseous.

A truck filled with animals slowed down as it arrived. The driver was a grey-haired man with a cowboy hat and his wife was wearing a tasselled coat. They were terrified, shattered, disconcerted. We went back to the auction site. I'd had enough of that damn zoo, of those cattle all over the place. I slept all day like a mad person, where the low-grade, germinating oats were going mouldy along with the bales of hay.

After a life of animals with my father, it was a life of fruit with my mother, in another little town, beside another highway. And the beginning of the epileptic seizures. It was after my father's death that foam came to my mouth and to the head of my penis. Suddenly, just like that, beads of a kind of white liquid began to form around my orifices. Before it dribbled out, I would feel I was playing with my life; I was ecstatically happy, I was shrinking and growing again. I would receive a voltage overdose. I was prey to a violent discharge, an electrical storm in my penis or my brain. But the ejaculations, at least, I could bring on. The epilepsy came less often, but when a seizure did come I would hide, in hay if possible, and let myself be overwhelmed. It would possess me, it was the opposite of a rape. I was attacked. I lost all control. I had to let myself be taken, like the girls who have no choice but resignation. Afterwards I go to sleep, exhausted.

CHAPTER 18

Rape is a game. You have to find the right players or everything goes wrong. It's a role-playing game. One day you buy your groceries, the next day you follow a girl, tie her up and have her. You threaten her with a knife, rape her, then hurry up and go home so you won't miss *The Simpsons* twenty minutes later on TV.

When I think of the rapes I've done, I take note of the hitches in the way things went and take steps to correct them before the next one. For example: at Ariane's I lost a lot of time cutting the tape with my teeth and my knife. If she had got excited, I would have stabbed her in the heart. I was overexcited and the adrenaline was pushing me to act fast. I had no time to lose. I thought of scissors for next time, then I had a good idea: handcuffs. That would fix everything double-quick.

When I rape, I break someone down by being as close as possible, to her, in her, against her. Sometimes I'm so carried away, so happy to project my being into a body that, really, it could almost not be a girl's. The other's body moulds to my brutal impulses, adapts to my ardour and power. When I'm on the point of an epileptic seizure, the prison guards put me in a cell entirely lined with rubber. Even if I try to smash my skull, throwing myself this way and that against the walls, I can't; I bounce off like a ball. The elastic room reminds me of a body I've broken into.

A rape is also like an epileptic seizure with the feeling it brings. A feeling of pure power, of loss and despair come over me and I have to carry through to the conclusion of the rape or seizure, sometimes in spite of myself, because people expect things to take their normal course. I have to get a hard on and rape, and I have to let the seizure invade me without resisting and wait till it finishes.

An epileptic seizure and an orgasm are alike in several ways. In both, a moment of suspense induces joy and envisions pleasure. Tremblings, abandon, helplessness, unusual strength, hardened muscles, agitation. It all ends with the discharge of a white liquid: foamy drool or milky semen. Next, for three seconds, sadness and shame take over. The body recharges. There will be another time.

With Ariane, everything had to be interrupted. A guy arrived, and I took off. It was probably her house-mate. I left Ariane's room as soon as he went into his. He came out and chased me, not knowing Ariane was lying tied up on her bed. We ran along the deserted street, cheeks burning from the sharp November cold. A moment came when I turned around to charge at him; I took out my knife. He gave up and went back. At the first corner I turned right. I didn't know where I was any more; I tried in vain to remember the street names I'd memorized while following Ariane. I was lost in this unfamiliar neighbourhood in Montreal East. Caught in the labyrinth, I had to ask a woman how to get to the métro station.

CHAPTER 19

Today is visitors' day. Maria will turn up, with her hair a little longer each time. She's promised to let it grow until I get out of here. I haven't told her yet, but it's going to be sweeping her ankles by then because my stay under lock and key will last sixteen years. That's what they decided at the trial.

She'll bring letters from my Uncle Tio, who's living in a hut on an island now. He and I talk about girls. He lives with two young orphans, two mini-hookers of twenty or so, that he keeps in exchange for small favours. From what I know of him, he must get himself sucked at least five or six times a day! He always writes to me in French, with his left hand, the one that's still intact. The girls write copies of poems by Rimbaud, which he includes in his letters. I've told him all about the rapes. He knows I'm in prison. I'd rather he send his letters to Montreal, though. I'm too afraid someone will read them here at the detention centre. Now, *he's* raped some girls! But in a context of war, it's different. It's tactical: the soldiers are supposed to sow their blood in the bellies of the women of the country they've attacked. They can also kill them after, if they want. It's their choice.

In his last letter, he talked about a journey to Asia. He knows important people, my Uncle Tio. One day, with his important friends, he went to eat sushi on a Japanese nude.

"She was transparent, with purple veins. Her hair on her head in a chignon was so shiny you could see your face in it. Her skin exhaled a lively scent of *saké*. Wasabi was spread across her hips, as far as her hairless mount of Venus, which was swollen with red tuna.

Ginger covered her boylike breasts completely. Only the discreet blinking of her eyes showed us that she was alive. Our tongues sucking up the cold fish from her pubis drew no expression from her. Delectable rolls of salt sea-weed, roseate flesh like a woman's open sex, the bitterness of tender flesh; there also on her stomach as flat as a palm leaf was that blue-tinged octopus spread out like a star, circled all about with scallops, sesame on her feet that were as long as my hand, whitefish and avocado slices on her thighs, halibut in her palms, and some shrimps between her languid fingers. It was cannibalesque."

My uncle always adored girls, to the point of wanting to eat them.

There was a note at the bottom of the page: "I'm sending a parcel with this letter–three volumes. I've wanted to introduce you to Sade for years. Enjoy, Mino."

It must be very early, five or six in the morning. I can't sleep any more. I had an epileptic seizure yesterday, and Dr. Parker gave me sleeping pills. I must have been lying in a bed at least fifteen hours. At first, there was Nurse Smith at my bedside. I tried resisting sleep so I could look at her and breathe in her smell of sweat. I like going into her little prison-nun's office because it smells of her. She's there bustling about, cleaning small instruments and filling her cotton-batting container. Sterile alcohol fumes mingle with her moisture and I hear glass things clinking together without breaking as I wait naked behind her. Knocked out by the medications, I'm asleep before she turns around.

I dreamed so much last night that I feel as limp as if I hadn't slept at all. My first dream was about escaping and being as light as air. It's an anonymous dream; all the prisoners must have it regularly. My feet barely touch the cold prison floor, they bounce me so high. I'm in a weightless state and I'm the only one who's this way. I flap my arms and realize that I can fly more naturally than I walk. My lungs are two air bubbles and my bones are made of foam. The prisoners watch me from their cells, mystified. I'd like to tell them I have no idea what's happening to me but my elastic leaps have already taken me far away. The speed of my movements is the only thing I haven't completely mastered yet, but that will come, I feel. Guards have been called. They chase me, jumping to grab my heels (I'm moving horizontally now, face down, parallel to the horizon). In front of the next door, Dr. Parker is waiting with a giant butterfly net. My head hits the prison ceiling and the roof detaches and rises toward the sky. Everything I touch is freed of the law of gravity. It's not Canada outside any more; I'm in Guatemala. Things have changed since I left for North America. The houses have been rebuilt, and I can't find my own. At this height I risk colliding with the speckled birds flying around me with small, bright-coloured crabs in their beaks so I come closer to the ground. Waking up is brutal–as if I'm falling from way up high into a bottomless volcano and only the end of the dream can shorten that interminable fall.

My second dream is chock-full of dazzling colours. There's Nurse Smith but when I look carefully I see it's my mother. There's Dr. Parker too, but his face is really Egg-pate's. The people around me have changed their heads with others, though they've kept their own voices and personalities. We're inside the prison and I've turned Nurse Smith's office into a fruit and vegetable stand. Strawberries repose in the cotton-batting containers, melon seeds replace the pills in the medicine jars, and I've stuck grapes on the syringe needles. On the table where one shivers naked while waiting for the nurse who's laughing on the other side of the mirror, there are tonnes of ripe fruit: papayas, pineapples, bananas, cantaloupes, mangos, lemons, guavas, coconuts, avocados, and hearts of palm. Maria arrives with Ariane and four raped girls. Maria has Ariane's body and vice versa. Guessing who has whose body is easy in their case because I know Maria's body well and Ariane has a ring in her belly button.

I explain to them how to tell if a pineapple is ready to eat. "First you must slap the fruit with your hand. If the sound you get is firm and short, it's a good sign. Yellow pineapples taste better compared to white ones which are not as sweet, though they can be used in cooking for tenderizing meats. When a pineapple is ripe, you should easily be able to pull out one of the leaves at the top. On the other hand, it's a good idea to keep some hard pineapples on hand. If a rapist hides in your apartment you can throw one at his head and you'll probably have time to get out before he comes to."

The girls think the joke is hilarious. It's attacker-victim humour. Maria asks me if I have any pomegranates so she can stuff them.

I say, "No, but you can always try with lemons. My little *criollos* are juicy and sweet."

Suddenly everything goes wrong. There are syringes instead of tender centres in the hearts of palms, the avocados have balls of cotton batting inside them, pills disguised as melon seeds spread a chalky kind of powder over the orange cantaloupe flesh, then Ariane chokes on a key while eating a papaya. It's the key to the handcuffs, which are inside the coconut I'm trying to open with my knife. The smell of the fruit is destroyed by the sterile fumes of medical alcohol blended with acrid emanations from the nurse's armpits. End of second dream.

Tired out, I rest in the middle of my prisoner's bed, which has never felt so uncomfortable, and fondle my penis to see if the medications' effect is still as deadening as ever.

CHAPTER 20

All my hope lies in the hollows of Ariane's hands. Spread over her palms, twisted around her fingers like thousands of wires. I wouldn't mind becoming her marionette. Being Ariane's puppet. Obeying her like a trained horse, like a stallion with a porcelain head and flexible legs (and a mega-penis like the Andalusian's). I would become her personal animal; I would obey only her, and people would see that Ariane is something else.

To Maria, I'd give a mean little kick so she'd go play in some other yard. Move her out, send her packing to way-off fields.

Maybe it's because I haven't raped recently that I'm obsessed with Ariane. Ariane, an epileptic seizure interrupted just before the climax. Ariane was too active, not playing her role as prey, putting up a fight instead of letting herself be led. I had to stop her, this Ariane who screamed, who laughed when she saw me leave her room. I had to convert her insolence into fear so I could turn back into the predator I am.

Ariane with her wide, questioning eyes. She's pulling on a thread, wanting things to take their normal course, and urges me on though I'm not keen. The kind of girl who insists on driving the car and ends up doing it better than you. She doesn't say where we're going and looks only at the road, smiling mysteriously like someone preparing to play a trick on you. Furious but saying nothing, you pretend to be taking it in stride. You announce the engine's overheating.

"Shut up, you little jerk," she replies.

She slows down as soon as a sign appears that reads, "Dump." I've never seen that word and ask her what it means. She snickers, chortles, laughs, splits her sides, sheds tears of hilarity. It's an abattoir dump. The black waves of putrefaction envelop me and I suddenly think of Nurse Smith.

"You're surrounded by a crown of abscesses and smoking anthrax," Ariane points out, sitting on an immense bull's head.

Her comfortably squeezed thighs are creasing the brow of the beast, whose unseeing blue eyes were dimmed with fear fixed in them. A ring hangs from his nose, like a magnified image of the one at Ariane's belly. The sun strikes their jewelery and reflects onto the dandelions. Ariane stretches out awkwardly, her shoulders behind the bull's horns, and taps his cheeks with her palms. It's damp here. Mauve intestines and brown blood, white eyes and hairy heads, little hooves like so many stones, and revolting nodes swollen like puffballs, which Ariane bursts because it's fun.

"Have to put lime all over, or things'll get infected." For the moment this is all I can find to say. Ariane has left me speechless, voiceless too, she sawed off my tongue with her cruel Sunday strolling. The girl is full of courage and barbarity.

"Have you ever played soccer with a calf's head?" she asks at last. She kicks one straight at my belly and splatters me with liquids red and kind of green. "Guess how many blobs of blood there are on your coat now," she demands.

She invents games whose aim I don't get and amuses herself making fun of me, and the calf, and the bull. There she is now, pulling on a purple, viscous rope, a long rubbery intestine. She ties it to the bull's horn and slips the other end in my hand.

"Come on, turn it! I feel like skipping rope."

She jumps very high into the air and each time she comes back down there are wet, squelching sounds. I'm sprayed with white and red globules. She doesn't weary of it, waits for me to own up to being tired and sick of it all.

"You know what?" she says finally, slowing down. "Under us there are lots of bones. Next event: finding the longest one."

And with that she dives into the slop and emerges triumphant a few minutes later, a sharpened rib in her hand.

"Torrès, come here," and the rattling of keys in the lock of my cell....

CHAPTER 21

I feel it coming, ready to explode, like an ejaculation. Its aura warns of the approaching implosion. My penis is stiff at last. Nurse Smith will take me into her office after the seizure, like a mother who's been awaiting her runaway son. Her immense bust will hang under my throat and my penis will point in the direction of her crotch while she slips tongue depressors into my mouth. It's when she pokes in my ears with her little instruments that her armpit comes right under my nose. Sometimes the smell is so sharp I'm suffocating with it, as if something's burning.

I'm going to take this seizure alone, quietly in my bed, and turn my head to the side to spit out the foam that will come to my lips. A rape goes like this. My only real fear when I raped was going into seizure. The intense excitement, the tumultuous outbursts, that mad, uncontrollable frenzy that takes hold of me during seizures and rapes are all so much the same.... The convulsions would have broken the rhythm, I would have lost control, I would have been ashamed to ejaculate foamy saliva through my mouth and collapse from fatigue. People expect things to follow their normal course; girls who are raped expect the attack to be finished. You've got to do what you intend and not let yourself be distracted, not think about the epilepsy. Because thinking about it too much brings it on–you let it know you're expecting it and it comes on you, like a premature ejaculation.

I shake a bit and my body stiffens. I've got my penis in my hand like a knife. I smile, ready to sink into the great void.

PART TWO
ARIANE

CHAPTER 1

Hamburg lay before me, legs spread. From a tower, I saw the sex-shop neon signs light up one by one as the sun went down. With my forehead glued to a bubble window, I watched in amusement the birth of startling yellows, garish pinks, and flashing greens, all excited by their own automatic movement. A boy threw himself into space at the end of an elastic cord, slashing vertically through the panorama. I watched his fall and his bounce back up, his less and less spectacular up-and-down, his arms always very straight, slicing the air and scorning gravity in the cloven sky. Six church steeples, some truncated by wartime bombings, rose like so many phalluses at the ready, offering to my eyes the toppled strength of a fragile Germany. Since the preceding November 4, I had been getting early-warning signs of desire overflow everywhere I looked.

A French tourist asked the elevator attendant what Hamburg was celebrating this May 7 to explain all the activity going on in the port.

"The city is celebrating the anniversary of the port commemorating the concession by Frederick Barbarossa, in 1189, of the right to navigate freely on the Lower Elbe. The exercise of this right, which was threatened by piracy and the feudal pretensions of other riparian claimants, notably Denmark, demanded surveillance by the authorities of the city which could not be relaxed until the 17th Century." This was delivered in impeccably articulated language. "Rowing freely on one's own waters, safe from pirates, calls for vigilance," the attendant added, directing a discreet smile at me, topped by a professional wink.

Walking down to the port, I spied a precocious young teen and her dishevelled dog. Snub-nosed, navigating self-consciously in high heels, Lolita was doing battle with a gob-stopper and at the same time playing seductress, throwing come-hither glances at sailors. Traces of the candy were showing at the corners of her mouth and she was grabbing flowers that appealed to her as she passed for the pleasure of making the most incongruous bouquet, when suddenly a mother's voice called, "Hildegard!" Lolita jerked her huge animal to a stop, her tight turquoise pants revealing the body of a child. She turned, thrust her bouquet into my arms, and like a small wet frog returned to her mother.

Anchors three times my weight were dangling their shadows down the hulls of ocean liners.

When travelling and hungry, I'll sometimes look around at the crowd or the customers in a restaurant and pick on someone, just like that, for no reason, and say to the waiter, "The same thing as that man." At the end of the meal, I ask the name of the dish and make discoveries. That evening, I'd chosen a rough-looking sailor with a scarlet face. I was expecting to eat meat or fish, something with lots of protein that you chew noisily and wash down with wine that stains.

An elegant woman passed with an undulating walk on the way to a green-painted booth. Intrigued by whatever it might be that she would want to ingest down at the port before going to the theatre or a concert, I abandoned the sailor and redirected my path to coincide with that of the lady with the orbital hips. I waited behind her, deeply breathing the honeyed fragrance of her perfume, and I too left carrying my cappucino with rum and my eel soup.

The tables were big upturned tubs that gave off salty odours. I dug my spoon into the grey-green bouillon, which left me puzzled, and rolled the eel on my tongue, surprised at its velvety texture and discreet taste, then my teeth tore the piece of milky flesh. A fiftyish man was surveying my profile and smiling. His eyes navigated my contours, roamed around my person, reeled about my thighs, preventing me from concentrating on the subtle flavour of my sea-serpent soup. Ignoring him wasn't the solution; he seemed on the point of approaching. I turned and stuck out my tongue at him, displaying a pulp of fish and other teleosts that his insistent presence was preventing me from enjoying. He moved away while I was imbibing my first sips of still piping-hot coffee.

In my pack there were some men's clothes. Before I left, my brother's girlfriend had given me a hat, some sunglasses, and a trench coat.

"Yes, Isabelle, but there's no more room in my baggage."

"Roll up the trench coat and squash the hat, that's all. Sometimes it can be very useful to pass yourself off as a guy."

I'd been in Germany for three days and already I was seeing a use for Isabelle's grandfather's old clothes. Turning myself into a man was the key that would allow me to venture into Hamburg's slimy lane, the Reeperbahn. Whereas Amsterdam devotes a whole district to vice, Hamburg concentrates all its vices along one artery. When I tried to go there the night before, I had been bullied by a prostitute in high spike heels and another had poured a cupful of urine over me. While I washed my coat at the youth hostel, I had made plans for this evening. I had invented a character; I would play a skinny little fellow who was embarrassed about going to see the hookers, wore his rumpled clothes stiffly and, from behind big, ridiculous glasses, avoided the eyes of women looking at him. The hookers must often see types like that.

This evening I would get in. I would put on my disguise and stop wondering if a man was following me, a bit like times I've crossed through the gay village in Montreal. With the impression of not being of interest to anyone, going incognito, persona grata (more or less), and less likely to be followed. I have these crazy notions, these beliefs that aren't really logical but that reassure me anyway. And since last November I've been cultivating all the things that neutralize implosions, even fans in winter. So "sex," the word in the forefront on every sign in the city, should cease to be only a term translated into a thousand languages. Henceforth it should have a smell, a colour, and I should know its obscene behind-the-scenes. I tapped on the bottom of the glass to slip the cappuccino foam into my mouth and looked around for a place to change in.

Decked out as a man, I set out for the Reeperbahn. It was 10 p.m., 4 p.m. in Montreal. Knowing it was still light in Quebec reassured me in a way, as if Hamburg's red light district were only an imaginary place, a theatre set. There were clues to show me I was getting close. On the postcards, church steeples, fish, and cargo ships had been supplanted by scantily clad women in stridently coloured lace. Widespread thighs painted on the doors of a bar announced that pussy was to be found within. In spite of my man's disguise, I had never felt so much a girl. A world was opening straight ahead.

A sticky smell of moisture rose to my collar and made me feel sick. Queen Pornography had damp armpits. My feet stuck to the street at each step. More and more women, breasts squeezed high in lustrous bustiers, were strolling about though not leaving a well-guarded territory. A sex-shop window was decorated with a circle of double ringed dildos with integrated lights, like a Christmas wreath. Here, sex had passed the threshold of temptation and was wallowing in ostentation.

Flashdance, Dirty Dancing, and other hits of the '80s were providing rhythms for the hookers to swing their hips to. If I were one of them looking at me, I'd have said to myself: Well, there's a nervous, scared little pervert who's got a hell of a hard-on and would love to get it inside one of us, and I'd feel ridiculous. I pushed my glasses further onto my nose and looked up. At a window, a tall, Spanish-type lady draped in a red dress was rolling her hips. I'd say she was forty, maybe more, on account of the tiny silver threads throughout her hair. She was taking flamenco poses with arched back and thigh-high slit in her skirt. She looked at me, trying to hold my gaze; I avoided hers. With a heavy accent, she said something like "lesbian," and I moved away.

I was surprised by the atmosphere of open camaraderie reigning here. The men were talking among themselves and laughing heartily. Sailors could be seen in deep conversation with hookers taller than themselves. Except for a few, the prostitutes were rather lovely. They looked like superwomen, with interminable eyelashes, breasts as round as balls hoisted up to their collarbones, their arched backs, their shapely legs, the artificial beauty spots on their cheeks, and their dark hair. No one seemed to feel any guilt for anything whatever; the men hung around in the lane, telling each other that Felicia was something else, but Andy's blowjobs were the best.

People were talking mostly English and German, with some funny, screwed-up accents.

Back to the youth hostel, in shock.

CHAPTER 2

I'm coming home from a poetry class, particularly stimulated today. It's half past five, the door's not locked and my cat comes out as soon as I've opened it a crack. I hurry to put on the new Portishead CD I bought this afternoon near the university. I take off my earrings, splash my face with cold water, pick up the messages from the voice box, and put some frozen pizzas in the oven. Back in my room, I lie down on my bed, curl up under my puffy goosedown comforter, and find two quarters under the pillow. The door to my closet is ajar; I get up and close it. The telephone rings. It's my brother, we talk for ten minutes or so.

"Alex, I have to go on account of synthetic pizzas on the point of burning to a crisp."

Before going to the kitchen, I turn on the TV to hear the 6 o'clock news. End-of-program credits on all channels; I turn off the set, not suspecting that I myself will be making the headlines of the next bulletin. Start of the fourth song on the CD.

When I'm back in the corridor, a gloved hand is placed on the frame of the bedroom door. I observe that immediately an armed man appears, his head under a hood and his eyes hidden behind dark glasses. And I start to laugh, thinking this must be a joke played by a friend of my house-mate.

When you read a book or watch a movie, you're expecting the worst, expecting the bad guy to show up. In real life things don't go that way. You tend to take its triteness for granted, to have blind faith in people, dilute your watchfulness in the relentless flow of daily life. Yet truth sometimes takes life further than fiction would dare for fear of losing credibility. This at least is what I realized that November 4, 1997. I asked the guy what he was doing here, suddenly seeing a knife in his hand. It was already too late. He jumped on me, angrily.

A blow to the corner of my eye, the knife handle hitting me high on my cheek, almost in my eye. I didn't know what violence was, I have trouble saying it even now. Before telling the police what happened, I had to search in the dictionary for words to describe what he'd done to me. At least there are some impressive-sounding words: creamed proboscis, (sounds like an haute-cuisine seafood soup served at a fancy banquet), haymakers and larrupings with haematomas (implying ouzo-marinated rabbit and mushrooms), whole face contusion, lesions of all kinds and blood pissing from my nose (understand tenderized rare *médaillon* of veal), and for dessert, words ending with "ing": shaking, dabbing, hurting; there, I'm ready to be served (floating islands with raspberry sauce). So, I've been cooked–now am I going to be eaten?

I still don't understand what it's all about. In a lane, sure, I'd have interpreted the scene differently, but in my apartment.... I'm too busy wondering how he could have got in to concentrate on how he locked the door with his gloved hand. It's my house-mate's fault, he must have left it unlocked. And I'm the one who's going to pay for it.

He throws himself on me again, this time from behind, his knees against the backs of mine. Now I'm threatened by a knife pressed against my throat. I let myself be plucked like a spoiled apple. At this precise moment, I imagine myself lying in a blood bath with my throat cut and my attacker astride me. I'm struck by an impression of unreality, I'm a character from those Bret Easton Ellis crime novels set in some seedy neighbourhood of New York. I exist in the plot of a fateful story that is not really mine: I no longer have a hold on my own life.

Perhaps a thief was caught by my arrival and wants to get away with my computer and electronic gear; cooperating is the thing to do, the knife and all that rage he's throwing in my face show me that in spades. He binds my hands behind my back and covers my mouth and eyes. Hampered as he is by his leather gloves, I hold back from laughing at him. Clumsily, he puts the tape in his mouth to cut it with his teeth. He gets impatient and tries to cut it with his sharp knife, though hesitating to let go of my hands (with reason, because in a flash I'd be up and away). Behind him, a jar of pencils with scissors in plain view. I smile inwardly, imagining myself offering them to him. It takes a long time, he's clumsy and my composure contrasts with his awkward, loutish agitation.

CHAPTER 3

I kicked about in the baroque gardens of Hanover with two Australian girls I'd met at the youth hostel. The place was crawling with strange characters who would have gone well with the hazy monsters of my childhood nightmares. Giant flies were moving to the sounds of Tibetan instruments whose guttural music gave a surrealistic twist to these gardens where Wagner or Beethoven would have been perfectly in place. Three fat, sixtyish Englishwomen strolled about, endlessly gurgling comments like, "Absolutely gorgeous" in their melodious voices.

A red apparition on stilts approached a child and caught him tight between his wooden legs. The kid howled but for naught; the monster was waiting for him to stop. Tousled and scarlet-faced as if the apparition's colour had stained him, the kid managed to break free. This was nothing like the cheery good-will of Mickey and Minnie Mouse, with smiles grafted onto their faces. I was observing the crying child and his laughing parents when a shudder of terror shot through my spine: to stir up some fun, a man disguised as an ill-intentioned fisherman had just given me a swipe in the neck with an eviscerated fish. But for me there's no fun any more with necks.

At the end of the avenue lined with lindens there's a high cedar maze. We took it on, smirking because we thought it was child's play... and spent two hours in it.

I began by losing the Australians, realizing that this supposed child's play was dizzying. Back in the middle for the umpteenth time, I had a spell of vertigo. I was unable to tell which path I'd arrived by. Everything was symmetrical; there was no reference point at all, not even a weathervane or a trash bin.

One's sense of direction is rather like one's confidence in people: you have to lose it in order to grasp how important it is. And if by chance you find it again, the state of deficiency is filled by an equilibrium and not delight.

CHAPTER 4

He throws me on my bed and shoves my face into the pillow. I can't get enough air and I can't see. Sitting on my back, he asks if I live with someone. He wants to know if I have a car and a credit card. I don't have any of that, you dumb shit. All you had to do if you wanted to fill your pockets was go to some big businessman's place in Brossard when he was out for the evening. This reminds me of those awful visits to the dentist who threatens the inside of your mouth while asking you questions you can't answer because you mouth's wide open. Except that right now I'm being made to keep my mouth shut.

The attacker stands up, repeats that if I do all he asks, things will go fine, "and don't forget I've got a knife." He has a Spanish accent and is really worked up. Wandering about jerkily like a snake in a cramped aquarium, he asks where my wallet is. I curse to myself because all I have is around two dollars in small change. I don't understand. Why's this scumbag in my apartment?

He turns my school backpack upside down and is furious not to find anything worthwhile. I think about escaping, figuring the distance from here to the door. I'll need a few extra seconds because with my eyes taped I won't be able to see where I'm stepping. Then, once at the doorknob, with my wrists taped behind my back, I'll need a few more to turn round and open the door. Mathematically, even counting on some reaction time from the attacker, this safety exit operation won't work because I'll have to pass him on the way. It's hopeless but I'm playing all or nothing. And it's at this moment that things really take a turn for the worse.

The CD puts rhythm into the scene, absurdly. I already feel like throwing up when I think about listening to it again. The attacker turns hysterical, grabs me by the scruff of the neck, and to the extent I can with my tongue imprisoned, I let loose a strategic howl aimed at the neighbours. They're there, I know. I can hear them walking around above, and I think I can make out the sounds of a quiz coming from the TV below. And my voicing takes a strange intonation. Normally, cries are spontaneous, loosed without intervention of one's consciousness. My voice bursts out like an S.O.S. in Morse code, a technical message risen from the furthest reaches of my throat. Yell as loud as I possibly can in hope of being heard, despair tearing at my flesh, breaking one or two vocal cords if need be. The long, still-born cry of a mermaid whose tail has been shattered by an ocean liner's propeller. This long, screeching message ends with a question mark. A parade of questions jostle in my head, vibrating with a single voice fibre. Why me? How did he get in here? Should I play the victim or try to defend myself? He's got a weapon. Where's my house-mate? Did my cat suspect something? Did the attacker wipe his feet before coming in? Did he smell the perfume on my clothes? Why doesn't he just go with my computer and my TV? Can't he stop the Portishead CD that gives a sweet tone to this too violent scene?

He smells faintly of sweat. He's not wearing any scent. I don't know how everything would develop without my usual calm. All of a sudden I understand the reasons for a lot of things and with disgust foresee the possibility of a forced lay.

Staying passive isn't my style. A powerful punch on the back of my neck and several seconds' loss of balance: that's what I get for trying to escape.

"If you stay quiet, everything will go fine," he whispers in my ear, tearing a strip from my right arm with his too-sharp knife.

Get away. Try again. Logically, this is the only workable way out, fuck the rest. I'm very busy wondering how to spare myself the worst. The fear comes after, when you're able to evaluate what you've escaped. The fear that it's all happening again, the awareness of having had a close shave because of a detail. The fear of the obvious you don't want to face, that you're lucky to be alive, the fear of never being able to trust people any more, the fear when a childhood girlfriend you haven't seen in a while comes up behind you and covers your eyes and asks you to guess who it is. The fear of never being able to wear necklaces again, the panic when people you love hug you and hold on too long. The fear of clothes-closets. The fear of walking home alone. The fear of lanes and rows of cars. Your heartbeat quickening at least three times a day because of creaking sounds from a wall.

Get away, yes. I run, in a void as we do in nightmares. The attacker goes crazy, delivers me two, straight in the stomach (all I can do is take it, hands taped behind my back, wind knocked out of me) and leads me sedately back to my bed. There are bits I don't remember because of the pain. A warm blade against my throat. He's furious. Through the tape across my mouth, I ask him what he wants, as if I had any doubt. I'm restless, thinking only of escape. I'd like to disappear or not exist at all. My cooperation at first was to give him time to leave with my computer and TV, not to get myself beaten or raped. But it's too late now. How weak we are when deprived of our physical senses!

What if he's afraid too? He's sitting beside me and I try giving him several kicks in the back with my knees, without much success. I won't give in. I'd like to hurt him, but at this point he becomes desperately aggressive. He plants himself above my pillow and, to shut me up, applies his two leather-clad thumbs around my neck; uttering ridiculous squeals, he tries to strangle me.

Ten seconds too long underwater. Being held at the bottom of the pool by a stranger. The lifeguard is dozing. My cries are swallowed up in the water, choked back by the chlorine. People walk by, thinking we're playing, that this parasitic body clinging to me is just showing delirious friendship. While I'm drowning, the lifeguard is scolding a turbulent child.

Sitting in an electric chair, feeling my eyes ejected from their orbits before I reach death. Understanding the reason for the tape over my eyelids: to prevent two excavations in the middle of a ravaged face. No longer able to breathe, ten seconds now, ten seconds too much, because my mouth is taped, my jaws are locked, and my nose is blocked by a cold that's going round.

Being an astronaut and losing my oxygen tank in space. Getting back to the rocket but having nothing to inhale. Trying to catch handfuls of air, unsuccessfully. Being helpless and powerless. Hoping I'm playing in a bad movie, thinking that maybe this is a bad dream, not giving up. Wishing for the pool to empty in record time, thinking that a power-out could save me from the chair just in time, looking out the rocket window and seeing the oxygen tank.

At best, this could be a dream within a dream.

CHAPTER 5

I was caught in a machination I couldn't escape. As soon as I moved, I got myself in deeper, fruitlessly spending my energy getting upset over it. Every time I thought I was coming to an exit, once again I found myself at the middle of the maze, with my calculations wrong. I had a mind to plunge through the line of cedars and, at the expense of getting scratched, at least be out of this numbing experience. The arrival of Maggie, who had chosen to laugh about it, calmed me. She talked about foxes hunted by fox hunting, in that elastic accent of the inhabitants of "down under." We took a path without thinking, talking, without trying to make a reasoned evaluation of our chances of getting out... and arrived outside in three minutes. Hannah wasn't there. I stayed near the exit we'd come to, and Maggie shouted. We heard several exclamations of "Fuck!" and "Stupid game!" hypocritically muffled by the dense silence of the trees, and Hannah finally reappeared. Let's go, let's get out of here.

CHAPTER 6

A solution comes into my head. The right one. The only one. Pretend I've passed out. Go limp in the coils of the Serpent. Let him think I'm maybe dead. He stops strangling me, just in time. My ploy has saved me, I owe my life to my on-the-brink dramatic skill. The sixth piece on the Portishead CD is coming to an end. In the silence between that and the next song, I hear the neighbour downstairs flipping channels, a laundry soap commercial, the loud buzz signalling the end of a quiz time allowance, people clapping, the canned laughter of an American sitcom. The upstairs neighbour making the floorboards crack on the way to his bedroom, right over mine.

The knife is sunk in my right arm, as if nearly dying of strangulation weren't enough to dull my mind. I don't know if the weapon's clean, I can feel it slash my flesh, sink below the uniform tissue of my skin. The attacker waits before withdrawing the blade. I can feel its metal against one of my muscles. Reduced to remaining passive, without any chance of action except faking death, I can only feel and imagine the lacerated areas of my flesh. Warm drops of blood form on my arm, trickle down my forearm. I can feel them accumulating in my joined hands. My hands are full of blood and I don't want to stain my comforter. I don't know what to do with this spate of blood that's gathered in the funnel of my wrists.

So killing me is what it's all about!

Footsteps on the stairs leading to my apartment. The attacker gets up and I hear my bedroom door slam. In my forced but lucid blindness, I imagine two possible scenarios. It could be my house-mate. If so, the Serpent is hiding behind my door, flat against the wall, and is waiting. I try to call out, but my lips are stuck together. The second possibility has me speechless, has my heart beating a mile a minute. What if there are more than one? What if I got the beating of my life, and they raped me ten times, not just once? If that's the case, the door must have been closed by the attacker, who has gone to talk to his accomplices.

I'm afraid to die.

For the moment, I have to survive, keep my head above the foam of what's left of my life. If nothing has happened in exactly five minutes, it's because the Serpent has run for it. If not, he's behind the door and making plans for a horror movie. I'm in an unbelievably lucid state; fear and hysteria have given way to iron-clad reason. Or perhaps it's fear that, pushed to its extreme limit, has turned into clear-thinking. I count the seconds, and the old hippopotamus system comes back to me. One hippopotamus, two hippopotami.... All the way to sixty, five times over. It's long. The precision of a Swiss clock; my margin of error must be between three and six seconds at most. I like letters better than figures, sentences better than matrices, poetry better than algebra, but we don't always have the choice. It was *grand-maman* who taught me to count hippopotami. At first, I always confused them with rhinoceri and this made *grand-maman* laugh. Apart from the horn and the rough skin, they're both big grey animals you only see in zoos. And even then, not everywhere. I think I've seen a hippopotamus happy in a sea of mud at Parc Safari.

Is this what one thinks about before passing over to the other side?

Sixty hippopotami. I jump up and run. I reach my bedroom door, turn around, find the doorknob without getting clobbered. I run toward the apartment door. It's wide open but I hit my forehead hard on the way out. I can barely give a groan of pain with all the duct tape on my face. My head spinning, I go upstairs as fast as I can to the neighbour's. I don't know if anyone's on the stairs. And I'm feeling a strange kind of joy in the idea that I'm not dead, that I'm still dragging life along with me.

Knock! Knock! Knock!

"Who is it?" James answers in a singing, jovial voice. I knock with both wrists at the same time, weakly, and let myself slide down to the doormat. Fuck, I'm sure to have messed up the door with blood. I hear James saying goodbye to someone on the phone.

"OK, I'll be there. You can count on it. See you." I'd bet my bottom dollar: he's going to see the worst horror sight of his life and he won't sleep tonight.

I'd like to get him to take the tape off my mouth first, so I can finally breathe big gulps of air. But he starts by cutting the tape around my eyes, and panics when he sees that they're bulging and red, and already have blue rings around them. He shakes a lot and keeps repeating, "Oh, my God!" Next he cuts apart my blood-filled hands and goes to find antiseptic bandages to look after the wound. The cut is not very long but pretty deep. The bleeding is profuse; I'd like to yell with pain but my lips are still stuck together. James's white face and anxiety reveal a turquoise vein in the middle of his forehead. And I, face twisted in relief and horror, lie resting on the floor in the hallway of James's apartment, making my joints crack.

I have a swollen head, the skull of someone with Downes's syndrome. The damage done by the mirror is as bad as what was done by the knife. My face offers the full range of purples, from scarlet to indigo. I look like a lilac in flower. The buds outlining my lips make a little string of coloured beads. I didn't know that people could bleed from the whites of their eyes. Trying to observe one's own eye is exasperating, it's a difficult, almost impossible thing to do.

When he cut the tape over my eyes, James shortened several eyelashes. I think of my Aunt Louise, opening the door of her oven and standing back up, black with soot and less the hair on her face. I think of children's drawings. A sun with eyelashes becoming a Mrs. Sun. "Sun" in French is masculine but in German it's feminine. I glance at all the duct tape lying around on the floor, stained with blood and with locks of hair stuck to it.

I'm covered with bruises, a Picasso-type nightmare. With three Beauty and the Beast bandaids on my right arm. Picturing this image of me, I venture a cry of revulsion.

Me and my blood-filled eyes before my brother in tears. We're driving to Venise-en-Québec, where my mother lives, where I was born and was conceived. My mother and brother came to get me. I think they would have made the trip by helicopter if they could. I was lying on the upstairs neighbour's kitchen floor with a blanket over my head when they arrived at last. There was no way

I was going to enter my apartment again. I wanted my brother to pack my suitcase and come upstairs with my cat, and then I wanted neither of us ever to set foot there again. I stroke the short locks of hair that fall on the back of my neck. I'm going to tell my friends in literature courses that, with my red eyes, from now on I'm like the character with the "perforated eyes" in Anne Hébert's poems. Proud and dignified in spite of all, barely recovered from that fantastic state of extreme lucidity. I already revel in recounting my assault in its minutest details, with emphasis on my staging of my loss of consciousness. I'm a heroine. Lara Croft, Hochelaga-Maisonneuve version.

It must be 11 p.m. when we reach Venise-en-Québec. I don't remember much what I told them during the trip. I had that damn Portishead song stuck in my ear. We passed a burning Quick Chicken outlet and I smiled, thinking I wouldn't be the only one in bad shape the next morning. When I realized we were going to the hospital, I naively asked why. The psychiatrist talked about attempted murder by strangulation. After an examination, it was confirmed that I had no hysterical tendency, that I was almost in full health. If I'd understood it was really me they were talking about, I'd have taken that as an insult. Me and my cool in the middle of a tempest unleashed on my body, me, having dragged myself gagged and blindfolded upstairs to the neighbour's in spite of my taped hands and eyes, having laughed when a potential murderer popped out of my clothes-closet as I headed to the kitchen. Me, having thought to turn off the oven when I sent my brother out to "the scene of the crime." Of course I have no hysterical tendency, it seems to me that's obvious. When we passed the Quick Chicken again, I laughed. My brother asked me how I could be cheerful after all I'd just been through. I told him that besides not having died by a hair's breadth, my apartment could have gone up in flames like a brochette if I hadn't thought about the pizza pockets burning to a crisp in the oven.

CHAPTER 7

I was travelling south on board an ICE, a kind of German TGV, a high-speed train. With an almond-and-cream cake in my mouth, a German newspaper on my knees, and Tori Amos filling my ears, I was leaving Lower Saxony for Bavaria. We passed through Göttingen, the city of Lou-Andréas Salomé. Germany was green, green, green, sometimes bled grey by the Rhine, sometimes dappled with little russet-red houses, watched from on high by ancient castles.

A French couple sat facing me, no doubt believing that I didn't understand a word of what they were saying. It did me good to hear my language anyway. The girl was very beautiful: dark complexion, round face, full lips, abundant, almost-black hair falling halfway down her back. Raindrops were running down, streaking my window and I glimpsed graffiti in the background. The French girl's name was Catherine. A blue fog was congesting the mountains, which had their escorts of vineyards, lettuces, and fields of mustard. Throughout much of the journey, I was fighting sleep as if my life depended on it.

Because, since last November, going to sleep in public is the worst thing that could happen to me.

CHAPTER 8

In the days following the attack, no one knows how to react. My friends in Venise-en-Québec come to see me. Emmanuelle brings me a box of jujubes and behaves as if I'm recovering from pneumonia. I'm still in bed; she sits very close to me, lifts the covers up under my chin. The instant she touches my neck, I feel a distress I never felt before, that makes me think of an exhaust pipe run over by the tires of a car.

"D'you need some syrup?" she asks me.

"I don't have a cold, Manue."

Apparently she'd rather I have a disease, even a serious one, than what I've got.

Nobody seems to understand that I owe my life to a matter of timing, good reflexes, and the arrival of my house-mate, who has left for his native Lower Saint Lawrence since the attack. Faking my loss of consciousness, getting my second wind finally after the whites of my eyes burst meant I was still alive. My house-mate's arrival meant no rape. I'm not killable, spread the word.

Maxime, another childhood friend, comes to smoke a joint in my company before going to work. I can see that he's embarrassed, but we both explode with laughter when he comes out with:

"I hope my eyes aren't as red as yours."

Then my mother buys me the victim's kit: leopard-print scarf to hide my mangled throat, movie-star sunglasses, lots of marshmallow-caramel Laura Secord chocolates, vanilla cigarillos, a bottle of port, and a black box like a pager which, when you pull a cord, gives a strident screech–call it a proxy-screamer-for-gagged-girls–a modern member of the family of victims' gadgets: the rape-victim's whistle, the gag-victim's phony pager, the frightened woman's Cayenne pepper (she hurries along clutching a small canister, its contents an impression of potential defence). Might the rape of a mute girl be the perfect crime?

The next thing to become my appendage will be a gun. Because arguing with crazies doesn't solve anything. Because legitimate defence is a pipe dream. I'll point the muzzle of the gun at the rapist's temple and say, You're going to pay for what you were intending to do. First, empty your bank account. We'll drop by a florist's so you can buy me some dyed sunflowers, the ones that have purple stems and bruise-coloured petals to go with my battered face. Finally, I'll stick twenty needles in each of your testicles.

My mother and brother have taken time off work. They're careful not to leave me alone. I feel like reading an Astérix, they read one too, glancing at me over the tops of their books. Without thinking, I blurt out that I have a desire for lobster. My brother runs at once to the market to buy three. It's been like my birthday for three days, but everybody's sad. People avoid alluding to the attack, as if I didn't want to talk about it and would burst into tears. I sleep in my mother's arms with my thumb in my mouth.

"Venise-en-Québec Osteopathic Centre, Good morning!"

"Hi. Could I have an appointment with Olivier Ernaux for... for something kind of urgent?"

"A place has just come open. If you can be here at 11 o'clock...."

"I'll be there."

I walk along the empty streets of the grey downtown, my eyes all red. I pass my Grade Six teacher coming the other way. If he recognizes me, he must think I'm shooting something very strong or else my live-in boyfriend beats me. But I avoid looking at people. I'm a prematurely born child, precipitously thrown into life and open air. I have potential nodes of fear in my neck.

In the waiting room, people observe me hypocritically. A child asks her mother the reason for the colour of my eyes. The osteopath receives me, intrigued, and I give him the story straight off. My red eyes look unwavering into his; I know he has a daughter my age and that my tale will hit home. He looks away from my steady gaze several times; my story isn't an entertaining one. He listens with close attention to the first part of it over again–curiosity gets the better of him–but doesn't let me finish at my own pace; he presses ahead to be done with it, foreseeing no happy ending. I pick up with a recital of my physical woes, which ought to rouse him from his torpor.

"First, my windpipe feels like it's been bashed in, my arm hurts, but I don't imagine you can touch that because there's a cut in it. My right floating ribs are out of place because they were flattened by a knee. My whole face hurts, and my neck, and my back all over."

He pulls on plastic gloves.

"Put out your tongue," he tells me.

My tongue is caught between his thumb and forefinger and pulled out of my mouth. I laugh and ask him what the hell he's taking me for, it's about my bashed-in windpipe. I have a horrible vision of that other man–my attacker–in gloves not because of microbes but for anonymity. I feel a sudden fatigue, and repugnance for all the curiosity about my face, which is black-and-blue and swollen all over.

A coffee in an ugly, empty restaurant, then I hurry to get home because my mother and Alexandre will soon be back and I don't want them to worry about my not being there.

After spending a week in the bosom of the family and with friends, I come back to Montreal, to finish the term at least. Just to convince myself of my own strength, I announce to everyone:

"No maniac's going to make me flub my last year of BA." I'd like people to admire my courage. Certainly not have them hand me a cup of coffee with cream and say:

"Poor little dear, if he raped you, feel free to talk to me about it." Certainly not have old friends I haven't seen in two years call and, without even taking time to be subtle or considerate, say:

"Hi, it's Anne-Marie, how's it going?"

"O.K. You? Long time no see...."

"Hey, is it true you got attacked by some crazy guy who tried to strangle you?"

"Yes, who told you?"

"Was it the place where you had that big Hallowe'en bash?"

"Yeah."

"Seems it was your house-mate that saved you."

"Yes and no. But it's a long story and right now I don't have time. Gotta run, 'bye."

The vultures are drawn by my drama. Each time I tell the story, I hone it a bit, as a storyteller will, and I feel I'm giving someone a gift. I want to give my story to those I choose. I hate hearing it told by someone else, my mother for instance. The tone is never right. Everyone thinks I'm to be pitied; I think I should be admired. I'm the heroine. I was only the victim by default.

My brother has decided to move in with me indefinitely. To protect me, but also to reassure himself. Alexandre is terrified by the idea that something could happen to me again, by fear of my death. My friends Emmanuelle and Maxime, my mother, my brother, and I are driving to Montreal, gloomily. My mother has bought me new, honey-coloured pine furniture. She's told me that we'll change my bedroom, that Alex will take care of me, and if I don't want to go back to the university right away, there's no problem.

The apartment is grimy with lampblack fingerprint powder, filthy with dead leaves and mud–the police investigators didn't take off their boots–and reeking with the smell of stale smoke. My housemate hasn't set foot in it since the event. Some huge, probably genetically modified strawberries are rotting in the frig, and reposing in the garbage can are three empty packages of Export A.

CHAPTER 9

I'd just arrived at the Munich youth hostel, just off the Rotkreutz Square, and I had terrible lower back pains. The twelve-hour journey and changes of train with my heavy pack on my back had left me dead-tired. In the hostel kitchen, I came close to bursting into tears when I saw my pasta had burned. Then came this peal of good-humoured laughter, such as I'd never heard before and which I couldn't tell if it came from a man or a woman. I turned toward the origin of the androgynous voice; rarely have I seen a guy with such a handsome face. A Czech, I learned later. In the evening we went to a Biergarten for a beer with lemon. We were caught in a thunderstorm and, huddled under an umbrella, I and the man with features as delicate as a bird's kissed. And I longed to go and make love in all the cathedrals of Prague.

He didn't want to go with me to Dachau.

"I visited the Terezin camp in the Czech Republic, and that was enough for me."

I bit into his hair, which was red and tousled and hung below his ears, and with my lips covered his impossible smile and his grey eyes like a cat's. He would go and hang around the English gardens, reading *The Unbearable Lightness of Being* in Czech. His first name sounded like a deep inward breath. Ihmre.

I left the hostel early so as to stop by the post office before catching the subway. It was raining heavily and a foggy humidity clung to my bones. Walking down to the Rotkreutzplatz, I trod on a twisted clothes hanger near the sidewalk and what a fall I had! Lying full-length with my head almost immersed in a muddy puddle and my right palm cut open, I laughed as I swore and my eyes were full of rainwater. I didn't even know how to say "bleed" in German.

"*Entschuldigung, meine Hände sind verletz....* Excuse me, my hands are wounded," I said to the attendant at a gas station. He brought out a first aid kit, picked the pieces of gravel one by one from the sore and applied a dressing to my wound, which was bleeding abundantly. I had a taste of ether in my mouth.

I set out again, hungrily eating an apple but revolted by long slugs that were crawling about on the wet paving stones. The terrestrial molluscs, wallowing in the humidity and offering their pale bellies to the hurrying feet of passers by, were sometimes crushed into a greenish purée.

CHAPTER 10

I don't have coffee with the downstairs neighbour any more. Guilt and an antihero feeling are eating at him, it seems. He heard me yell. I have to say I didn't yell much; only once in fact, when I was trying in vain to escape. A strategic howl, a bottle in the ocean, a desperate appeal to Someone, in case Someone was there to hear.

Now I find myself on the stairs meeting up with his girlfriend. She asks me how I am, perhaps trying to see the bright red of my eyes behind my sunglasses (I'm becoming paranoid, by pure logic, and I'm learning to suspect people). I don't know quite what to reply. If I'm OK, it's for one reason–I discovered my strength. However, fear mingled with silence gnaws at me. I can't stand being alone. I'm becoming a bundle of anxiety, features drawn, face ravaged by worry.

To the question, "How's it going?" I make do with a heartfelt "Not bad," and for once it's true; things haven't got worse for me.

I ask why her honey is avoiding me. It's because he feels guilty, the incident has shaken him, he's angry with himself, he's not proud to be a man, she explains fondly. Perhaps she expects me to reply, No, no, it's not so bad, tell him I don't hold it against him and I'm getting better. I can't. Things would have gone differently if he had intervened. It enrages me to think of him sitting in his armchair flipping channels at a time when there's nothing worth watching on TV, while I was sunk in near-death three metres above his head. I am the heroine and the victim too of this whole story.

People think I'm going from bad to less bad because my bruises are turning from purple to pink. But who watches the morbid, repetitive reruns that flash through my head? Several times a day, the film of my attack plays on all the channels of my inner TV. And when the film begins, I must watch it scene by scene until the end, then there's rest. The only trick I know to stop it is to open my eyes and say, "Stop!" out loud. And put on the light, even to sleep by. Specially to sleep by.

Who can guess how fear rules my solitude?

CHAPTER 11

Aboard the Strassenbahn–a little street train leading to the Dachau camp–I was urging myself to be compassionate, as if I was afraid of being insensitive to the world's most accomplished work of human destructiveness. I imagined the prisoners packed into cattle cars and ordered myself to be touched by the scene in their memory. I wanted to react with as much compassion as my house-mate. The attack on me so upset him that he told me he would never set foot in the apartment again, "and maybe not in the big city either." Queer kind of logic. Proportionately speaking, there are as many horrors in secluded villages–fertile ground for hidden iniquity–as in big cities. But he shares my fear, and that makes a little less for me to bear alone, one could say, and then, I call that showing empathy.

The place looked like a human-being farm. A parent couple had brought their two-year old kid, who was bawling hard enough to expel his tonsils. The harsh voice of a baby in a tantrum overhung the general murmur. I was astonished to see families. If I had a child, I'd show him Neuschwanstein Castle, not Dachau. An American woman was industriously and insistently filming the inside of a hut's washroom. In memory of the people who had suffered, her tactful spouse uttered cries and made sounds of movement that were supposed to reconstitute events from history, an American-style remake without the special effects. Bad taste to the power of ten. Pathological.

Before a road leading to the monument in memory of the atrocity stood a copper sculpture that attracted my attention. In it you could see, tangled together in a compact mass, prisoners as thin as wire and spiky barbed-wire. I was impressed with such aestheticism born of horror. A sentence from George Santayana's *The Life of Reason* captioned the spirit of the site:

"Those who cannot remember the past are condemned to repeat it."

Poppies dotted the ground where some prisoners had bled to death. The still-fresh wound to the palm of my hand kept jolting me, a stabbing pain like that from aluminum reacting with a lead tooth filling.

A small community of Carmelites had settled in the camp. The basis of their monastery's architecture was a cross that continued and terminated the main entrance road leading to the administration buildings. The nun's cells formed the arms of this cross and the cloister its head. The chapel was the body of the cross, the altar and tabernacle rising at its heart. I imagined the architect Joseph Wiedermann's face when he was asked to draw the plans for the Carmel of Dachau. Surely it must have been the same face made by post-war tattoo artists who were asked to turn swastikas into orchids.

At the left of the camp were the crematory ovens and the gas chambers. In memory of cremated prisoners, people had placed candles on the ovens. The heat from them was really unpleasant, the more since it was very humid outside. The heat abated when one stepped inside, bringing a feeling of relief... until one read *"Krematorium."* This section of the camp was isolated by iron fencing in geometric motifs. On the gate was the cynical inscription, *"Arbeit macht frei"*–"Work is freedom–a slogan recalling George Orwell's renowned, "War is peace, Freedom is slavery, Ignorance is strength" in his *1984*. Everything here left me with an impression of poorly coagulated healing, of fractured irony.

It must have been 2 in the afternoon. I was starving but too upset to eat. I was discovering contaminated ground in Germany that was surviving its vanished church steeples, its concentration camps that had brought rot to the cities, surviving its post-1945 history museums, and a collapsed and badly-healed wall. I was learning that Germany was not only the aggressor it was claimed she embodied. She also had a battered side, some open sores called Dachau, Ravensbrüch, Sachsenhausen, and Buchenwald. Weakened by her power, she was recovering from her post-war wounds and was stronger than before for having pondered her weakness in the red of her own eyes.

There was hardly anyone at the youth hostel. Suited me, what I really wanted was to take a hot shower and stay in it for 45 minutes. The spectre of what I'd just seen would haunt me for a long time, was already weighing heavily on my breathing.

The Czech had left a message on my pillow. He would be in the English gardens until 5 o'clock, near the Chinese pagoda. The message was in English and German. I knew no Czech, he knew no French; I spoke good English and got by in German, the other way round for him. But we managed to understand each other well in the creole we were inventing.

CHAPTER 12

I think about my brother's anger. Since the attack, Alexandre has been sleeping badly. That's why he's put three locks on each of the front and back doors of my apartment. He gets up early every single morning since the attack to put make-up on my face, giving it a coating of base to start.

"No, that's not right, it seems to make you look pale." Alex waits for the pharmacies to open so he can go and discuss these things with the make-up ladies. "This one should do it. It's Revlon; the other one, Maybelline, was oilier. I've bought you some eye shadow, too."

It's touching to see a tiny brush in his big guy's hand. More touching than to see a knife. Anyhow. His girlfriend has lent me a filmy, saffron-coloured scarf.

I'm alone in the apartment when the investigator informs me by phone that two other girls have been assaulted and raped by the same attacker as me. Strange, the effect of tears fallen into grey dishwater. My brother arrives around 6 o'clock bringing hot dogs and mustard with coleslaw from Valentine's. When he hears the news, he rushes to the bathroom, throws up in the toilet, and says he would rather have had all that violence directed at him. He also talks about his girlfriend. I think Isabelle has been raped, though Alex only touches on the subject. Pink around the mouth and his hair soaked with sweat, he sits on the floor with his back against the bathtub. I wet a facecloth in icy water and wipe his face and hair with it. We go to bed soon after. I give him a little white pill to put under his tongue to help him sleep, to stop the scenario that plays out over and over at lightening speed in my head and apparently his too. To show him pink elephants on unicycles riding on clothes lines in a Montreal lane.

"Take this tablet at bedtime, it's like a glass of white wine," the psychiatrist had said.

The next morning, the hot dogs are still there on the table. Alex comes to wake me, a plate of caramel toast in one hand and make-up base in the other. David Bowie playing in the background.

CHAPTER 13

Ihmre was smoking a Phillip Morris, his hair mingling above his head in the deep bark-grooves of the tree he had his back against. I watched him. He pulled blades of grass, scratched his stomach, rummaged in his mustard-coloured pack. For the first time, I noticed the fineness of his nose, its translucent nostrils rising and falling like the gills of a fish. He had emphasized his eyes with a line of pencil. I thought of my brother and smiled; I appreciated boys with a grasp of the rudiments of make-up. Though Ihmre wasn't effeminate, there was something feminine about him. He was the happy transition between man and woman, the brief encounter who was opening my eyes to strangers, teaching me to love my neighbour again. As I approached unseen, he drank some of his apple drink and bit into his bar of chocolate with almond paste.

"*Meine Liebste, wie geht's,*" he said.

"*Gantz gut!* Well... I found the trip a little traumatizing."

"*Ja. Ich verstehe.* Like I told you. But you have to see it to understand."

His velvety eyes made me want to fight a revolution with him, go and shout in Czech from the highest castle in Prague, become a scribe for Jewish history, swim across and up and down the Vltava, swallowing big mouthfuls of it, to exhaustion, and hang out in Venceslas Square. He had been robbed of *The Unbearable Lightness of Being* at the youth hostel and his sorrowful face was not without charm. I tried to tell him the end of the story from memory. He took my hand and when he kissed my palms was worried about my wound. Lying on the grass with my head in his lap, I fell asleep.

CHAPTER 14

I wake up exhausted from so much dreaming. Since my brush with death, I have been revisiting my childhood fears: horror of clothes-closets, fear of darkness and being alone, post-nightmare anxiety. There are advantages and disadvantages in my condition; at least everyone understands my fear. My brother has taken the doors off my clothes-closet and has moved in with me. When a nightmare comes, I don't have to run to my mother's room at the risk of some ghoul grabbing my ankles from under my bed; my brother's there, sleeping beside me. I squeeze up tight against his back, he breathes out deeply and says:

"No, I'll mow the grass tomorrow." I've just had a nightmare and he talks to me in his sleep.

The other day on TV, Claire Lamarche met with a group of survivors. They had survived illnesses, wars, assaults, suicide attempts; a fine gamut of cripples, in other words. Some returnees from death's door were so pretentious over their return to life! As if there were an exclusive fraternity with a secret sign identifying its members to each other. As if, all of a sudden, souls aged and pupils darkened. Of course, they had all seen their lives flash past their eyes and then the tunnel of light, and there was certainly no question of hippopotami or rhinoceri, oh no! They carped over the meaning of life and of its opposite, nothing less.

I hope my demise will escape that tunnel cliché, or I shall die in exasperation. From my own forced flirtation with death, what I remember is that fear, once beyond its paroxysm, becomes extreme lucidity. And that the eye can bleed.

To this survivor, all that life holds from now on is summarized in two words: sadness and paranoia. I'm talking here about a sudden disappearance of confidence in people, infinite sadness like a rat dead from AIDS in a velvet box, or the burned, bubbling stuff at the bottom of a pot forgotten on the stove. I'm talking about a reasoned paranoia that deserves respect, that is founded in reality and not in the twisted knot of a serious neurosis.

But in parallel, a new strength is settling in, and that strength can bring joy. What is the nature of this assurance and strange joy that spreads through one at the very moment when confidence in people evaporates and is replaced by the sadness of artificial lakes and suburban traffic lights? Better to be sad and strong than beaten up and weak.

The haven of daylight beyond my eventful nights is now being denied me. While the clothes-closet monsters go back where they belong when the first rays of dawn streak the sky, reality's monsters poison my life round the clock. So the man sitting in the métro station holding a bouquet of flowers may be on his way home to slit his wife's throat, though neither he nor anyone else suspects it. And who knows, the tall, skinny fellow who cooks Big Macs in McDonald's back kitchen could be a murderer. My attacker was selling fruit at the Jean-Talon Market and kept what the lawyer called a low profile: 23 years old, a wife and an apartment in Montreal North. The police arrested him recently. Not because they did their job well, used perspicacity or anything like that, no, no. He had dropped his wallet with all his identification cards at the third girl's place. Lounging in front of the TV in his living room, he never thought for a second it was the police ringing at the door.

"*¿Que passa mi amor?*" his wife perhaps asked in a musical voice from the room where she was cooking.

So I can't count on daylight or my apartment for refuge. Alex has left for work, and I try to read. It's windy outside; at the slightest creaking from a wall, I sprint out of there, not daring to set foot inside again. I go and knock at James's door and he comes and checks the place out and reassures me. I've been in the apartment since yesterday and my brother was here with me this morning. I know perfectly well there's no one else here but me, but–I'm afraid. My cat's soft little steps on the floor make my heart race. I hear the tiny sounds and rush toward their origin with my phony pager in my hand, ready to let it screech. Startled by my haste, the cat recoils, its tail between its legs.

I'm afraid. An illogical fear that defies explanation. When I'm alone it comes back to haunt me, like a stealthy ghost, a cold sore that keeps tormenting. As soon as a friend shows up it fades, stays quiet, and I'm reassured. I make those who keep me company bear the whole weight of my fear. These days they have to be built strong for that. I have red fireworks at the junction lines of my irises, against a whiter and whiter background. The wounds to my face, the bruises on my throat, my missing eyelashes, and the cut on my arm are tending to disappear. People keep telling me I'm getting better. As long as I'm not alone, I agree. Like two suicidal best friends who whoop it up every time they see each other, happy to be together and forgetting to talk about death; then each goes home alone and anxiety comes back at the gallop. When I'm alone, it's limpid, indefatigable fear that stretches out with me on my eiderdown, looks into the red of my eyes from the back of the microwave, sitting on my pots of Nutella, or lying curled up in a ball among my dirty laundry. Hypocritically, I play tricks so as not to hear those little creaking noises that get to me. At the end of November, I turn on the fan and appreciate its reassuring hum that muffles the plumbing sounds from the first floor, people's voices from outside, and little cat footsteps. But when I let it run too long it gives me a headache and I agonize over the thought of having to turn it off some day. Of being confronted with so-called silence. Then I turn on the dryer and manage even to laugh at myself.

I went to visit my friend Philippe, in the Village near the Papineau métro station.

"Your eyes! Is that going to go away?"

"It's already better than it was. I put a hot, wet facecloth over the lids for twenty minutes, morning and evening. I'm fed up with everybody looking at me. When I wear sunglasses it's worse. I look like I'm taking myself seriously."

"I don't want to insult you, but it's almost attractive. It makes you look a little vampirish. One kind of expects to see your canines lengthen when you smile."

"Did you know you could bleed from the eyes?"

"No, I didn't know that, and I still don't understand how anyone could have wanted you dead. Would you like me to massage your toes? It makes you feel really great, you'll see."

"I've lost confidence in my senses, Philippe. A crazy guy spotted me so as to.... I don't really know what he was going to do. Rape me, strangle me, beat me up, steal my money? I'm so tired of wondering about it all the time. Seems like there's no room for anything else in my head any more. And I thought I had intuition for things like that...."

"Come on, take off your socks."

I don't want a sound or a movement ever to escape my attention again. I challenge all my senses, putting them through rigorous training. I concentrate and can hear the blinking of cats' eyes, the beating of flies' wings, and hairs falling to the floor. I linger over invisible things: the details of dust crystals drifting about the living room on sunny afternoons, the colour of water and the humidity around me. Nothing is softer to the touch than Isabelle's saffron-coloured scarf, the flesh of crabs, and baking powder. I'm training my senses to detect all the defectives who are hiding themselves from me. I can smell the subtle odour of the sweat of shadows, and of cyclamens, and I'm drawing up a list of voluptuous foods:

– violet candies

– thai soup (curry, coconut, vermicelli, lemon grass, and onions, with a little lettuce in the bottom of the bowl)

– fresh-squeezed pineapple juice

– blueberry chocolate

– Munich figs (marinated overnight in brandy, wrapped in bacon, and oven baked)

– Hungarian cheese croquettes

– almond milk

– avocados

– dates stuffed with Stilton, Portuguese style

– salad of hearts of artichoke

I go into a café that has a flag with the seven colours of the rainbow over the door. Like cities, cafés can be sexed. The waiter calls me "Miss" in a cross-legged tone of voice. I like being the only feminine presence in the place. I order a rocky road cake with bananas, dark chocolate, and white chocolate on a bed of light custard. I have a new ring on my finger.

I was attracted by its colour, a true amber, on the way out of the métro. The ring was too small for me, which never happens because I have such slender fingers. The shopkeeper of African origin brought out a long metal tube and slipped the ring over it, hammering as if to force the ring to distend. For a moment it made me feel a little sick. I tried the ring again. It passed the stage of my second joint but resisted ¾ up my finger. It jammed there and I felt my ring finger swell. Frightened, I smiled as I fought to wrestle it off me. Or wrestle myself from it, I'm not sure which any more. In vain. I was grappling with this parasitic body that was attached to my person beyond my will. I turned red with anger, and tears came to my eyes. Helpless, I offered a hesitant hand to the shopkeeper. Pulling very hard, he managed to remove the ring, then took up his hammer again and worked at it for fifteen minutes. I wasn't at all sure I still wanted to buy it. I sat on the dirty métro stairs and chewed my nails like a madwoman. The shopkeeper gave me a little tap on the fingers when he saw the result. My hand shook, the ring was perfect. He began to laugh, an elastic and increasingly loud laugh.

"Oh, so you think it's funny!" I said, insulted. He took my hand and led me inside the little shop to a row of masks.

"Which would you like? You see that one, the one making the face? That's exactly what you look like right now."

A black mask, a long, anxious face, delicately lined. I chose it.

CHAPTER 15

A little while before, I felt how fragile the attack had left me. I went to buy some fudges for Ihmre and me. Vanilla ice cream coated with white chocolate or apricot sugar: surely an incentive for immigration to Germany. I was alone in the convenience store. The man at the cash was Greek; he told me he wasn't married and didn't often see girls like me. I looked him over briefly, frowning. He took my hand to give me my change. His nails were filthy and there were brownish blotches all over his face. When I pushed the door to go out, he was there, looking at me, and the door stayed shut. The bastard had locked it. I felt my legs weaken, my heart beating hard against my rib cage, my windpipe contracting, my eyes growing red with blood. I immediately spotted a cutting object with which I could do him serious damage: a bottle of wine. I'd smash it against the floor then clobber him in the nose, yelling in his ear, Unlock the door or I'll do the same to both your eyes! I was having violence fantasies; for all the nearly-strangled women on earth, I'd decided to make him pay. All this developed in my mind inside a single second.

"You S.O.B., you're going to open it," I said.

"Ziehen musst Du," he replied, meaning, "Pull, don't push."

At that, I confess, I got steamed. Just before going out, I cleared my throat and whole respiratory system, then spat on the doormat. For all, male and female, whose nerves are raw because of the hold some deviant has on them.

I asked Ihmre why he had come to Germany. Savouring his fudge, he talked to me about his Czech Republic, which had been invaded so many times by foreigners. A peaceable, harmless land raped by the Nazis, the Communists, the Americans, the tourists, his republic was recovering from its wounds as best it could. From Germany, he wanted to contemplate the strength, meticulousness, determination, the soul of a republic strong in good times as in bad.

A drop of orange-coloured fudge plopped onto my knee. Thinking again of the concentration camps, I asked Ihmre where such animosity came from and how the human species could arrive at the point of exterminating itself. Languorously, Ihmre licked up the sweet liquid that was thickening on my knee. No doubt he thought me a bit naive. Yet I had given up trying to change the world. I was just trying to understand how someone can get so he'll rape, kill, or orchestrate a war. I couldn't give up the "whys" that were gnawing at me.

Ihmre told me things in a random kind of way. About the time he'd visited a Czech concentration camp at Terezin. Near the Star of David that cast its shadow over the huge, anonymous cemetery, he had seen two or three neo-Nazis sitting on a tombstone, smoking a joint. He could not erase their self-satisfied smiles from his memory. About his four younger sisters, and his studies in the teaching of German, which he was no longer sure he wanted to continue. About longing to eat a nourishing meal and drink a bottle of syrupy Czech wine... and my big, serious eyes which he was already gazing into.

I imagined Ihmre in a black coat, without make-up, crossing a bridge in Prague on a foggy morning on his way to the university, flicking a half-smoked cigarette into the Vltava, where gothic, baroque, and spikey architectures blend in disturbing harmony, the one you find illustrated in books on Kafka.

As an antidote to the concentrated dose of hatred I had consumed in the afternoon, Ihmre and I could see only one solution–its opposite. We went and ate *schnitzelen* at the Türkenhof and afterwards attended an open-air classical concert not far from the city hall, drinking beer. Then we slept together at the youth hostel.

CHAPTER 16

I'm coming back from the university and I know Alex won't be home yet at this hour. I decide to go and see Geneviève and François who live not far from my place. I kid myself I really do want to see them. They're not there. Fuck. Strategy number two: pretend I'm dying of hunger and can't live without a poutine from Ginette's. Ginette's waiting only for me, 24/7, more faithful than a dog. Give me poutine cuisine, it's brought us the most genial of the junk food family. I pick up *Le Journal de Montréal,* eager to read, then change my mind. The front page headline announces: "Métro murder victim killed with hammer." I don't take kindly to someone having more bruises than me. The idea that I'm not an exception, that violence is alive and well, delivered gratuitously let alone in bitterness or hatred turned physical, gives me electrical shivers between my shoulder blades. I'm disconcerted by my former naivety. I was at peace in my mind, but so foolhardy. I turn the worthless rag over as I slip the first curds of hot cheese onto my tongue. More salt.

3:30. Alex must be back. I haven't even arrived when I feel tears dangling from the end of my chin: my brother's car isn't there. I know the upstairs neighbours haven't yet finished their day of work, and the one downstairs is hiding from me. I won't go in alone because I'm terribly afraid. Just at the thought of trying, a headache I know well since the attack invades my skull. I sit on the little fence while I wait for my brother and stare defiantly at passers-by, my hand on my phony pager. The sun beats down on me like an imbecile's good humour. I can still taste poutine in my mouth, I'm too hot in my coat, I feel sick. James arrives finally, an hour later, and invites me to have coffee with him. I accept and vent my anger against Alex. When we pass the door of my apartment, we hear footsteps.

"Come out of there, you damn fool," I yell, "that's my place you're in!"

My brother opens the door, his hands covered with pastry dough.

"What's got into you, and where were you? I've been looking for you for an hour. I called your friends, everyone's worried."

"Where's your car?"

"I lent it to Isabelle, she's got an interview in Sherbrooke tomorrow morning."

I forgave him because of his cherry pie. My brother makes lovely sweet desserts for me. We howled with laughter over this afternoon's episode. Then I said:

"I'm fed up with being scared and having headaches all the time. My house-mate's never coming back to Montreal, I've picked up my emails at the university, and now that's it. Alex, we're going to move."

A nice little apartment shaded by an old oak tree that was pruned by the ice storm. I'll live there with my brother. He's scared, scared for me, afraid something else will happen to me and I'll die from it. We moved in the middle of a snowstorm. The streets were slippery, and the back of the small van we'd rented kept skidding. I spilled a bag of cat litter all over the steps, not realizing the bag had a hole in it.

After the move, Isabelle suggested we go and have a beer at Les Foufounes électriques. My brother knew the waiter, a hefty guy with a roll of fat at the base of his skull, who was plainly fascinated by my red, white and black eyes. I bamboozled him into believing I'd made them that way with non-toxic food colouring and I was seeing red.

"Your sweater's black, I suppose," I said to him.

"Yes."

"It looks purple to me."

"Alex, your sister's all fucked up!"

That night, I sleep alone in my honey-coloured pine bed. I left my brother with Isabelle, not without a twinge of fear–this is my first time alone at night since the attack. To keep my mind busy, I read *The Chess Player* by Stephan Zweig while I drink a Second Cup hot chocolate, which sits a little heavy on my stomach. I try to distract my five senses, so they'll forget what was done to them. There's the Indian incense as well, and Chopin's Nocturnes, the soft blanket I'm cuddled up in (a temporary replacement for Alex), and my window open a crack so I won't suffocate. The cat's licking the cream filling from my Mae West. Oh well, with the hot chocolate the cake was getting too sweet anyway. The cat comes closer, stretches across my book and begins to purr. Anything to distract me. So I won't panic at the thought that someone tried to put an end to me in this bed.

I still can't sleep unless I take the little white pill that tastes like chalk. I need something that knocks me out in a big way, that cheers me, removes my worry, and lets me give in to sleep. Without that tablet, Lady Insomnia waits with wide open arms. And I'll go through a routine of calculations. Is the door really locked? Where's my phony pager? I'd like to have it beside me, but not directly in my line of vision because it will remind me of what I'm trying to forget. Am I a light sleeper? This question underlies another: if an undesirable comes into the apartment, how much time will I have before I'll have to wake up? And my head will ache at the temples from juggling frantically with all this.

I open my eyes around 11 o'clock and am bewitched by a penetrating smell of coffee and the sizzling of bacon frying in a pan. My brother and Isabelle are billing and cooing. I hear them giggling, Isa bursting into delighted laughter and my brother saying, "You're going to wake my little sister," then I pipe up to tell them I'm already awake. Good humour rules, Alex comes and tickles me in my bed, asks if I've slept well. I announce to him that I'm going to paint my room.

CHAPTER 17

We were crossing Germany from south to north. The train, which we very nearly missed, had left at 6 o'clock that morning. Now Ihmre was asleep beside me; it was 8:15. I was observing his slender hands, his long, piano-player's fingers. At the hostel the evening before, he had sat down at the piano as naturally as could be and played a movement of Dvorak's *New World Symphony.* I like people who have hidden talents, which they reveal at the right moment like that.

When he woke, we drank some train coffee and ate custard-filled cakes. The grey of his eyes was emphasized by blueish circles around them. I asked him to speak to me in Czech, a gentle language, but jagged in the corners. Not understanding the meaning allowed me to concentrate just on the musical sounds of the words he was saying softly, smiling. He wanted me to speak to him in French. Since there were two Quebeckers near us, I told him to listen a bit to them. He asked me to translate. "There are as many cows in Switzerland as scooters in Rome!" they had said. He kissed me on the neck and played with my hair. It was my turn to sleep. With him, I could fall asleep on a finger-snap. First time in months.

Ihmre woke me at 12:30 because we had to change trains at Nuremberg. I think I had dreamed in German and I'd dreamed I was having insomnia. We took a two-decker train and I passed through the city of the great trial like a sleepwalker.

CHAPTER 18

"Logically speaking, if this can reassure you, there's very little risk that you'll be attacked again. Statistics show that... hardly ever happens, we can reliably say not twice in a lifetime... not because of the way you dress, it could have been anyone else."

Thus speaks Miss Feet-on-the-Ground personified, the psychologist. I retort that this assault on my person was not an everyday, common-or-garden occurrence. I want people to forget logic in accounting for fate and stop trying to reassure me about the future. Because it's right now that I'm afraid. And I'd like to know my nearly-strangled sisters. To know why it was the three of us. Is it a compliment to have been chosen and desired by a rapist? I demand that my questions be answered. Above all that I not be told to strike up a conversation with my fear when it shows up.

If we have to go to court as witnesses, I shall be their strength. I shall arrive late at the court house. They will be colourless, he will be bilious green. I shall have the colour of a movie star, make-up by Alexandre, a blood-red wig to match my eyes, a padded corselet, long cigarette pants in form-fitting leather, and those high heels that give women curvature of the spine and ingrown toenails. I shall speak like an academic and shall tell the court that I have come to avenge femininity dressed as what is exceedingly ugly about it. Because femininity had something to do with these assaults. I understood this truth much later after the "why me" phase. With a knife, I shall scrape the flesh from his arms as he did to us. But down to the bone. I shall extract the marrow and put it in a little bottle, and order a batch of shampoo to be made of it. Lipstick is made from pig pancreas, after all.

The worst of this whole story is to have been attacked in my apartment. Worse still, in my own bedroom, in the bed I slept in as a child, which would have become a coffin the moment two eyeballs popped from their sockets. If I'd been near death in a lane, I would have hurried to get back to my territory, my little world, my room. But mine is a different case. I'd even go so far as to say I feel safest in the middle of the street, on the yellow line. Certainly not at home. I hesitate to lock the door in case someone's already inside. I make logical calculations and reach neurotic little conclusions. If I have to run for it, the locked door will delay me a few seconds and might allow a stealthy madman to get hold of me. And besides, if the neighbours heard me and tried to get in, they couldn't, or it would take them too long. My heart beats wildly, as if it's trying to break through my rib cage and come whirling out to mince up the air I'm trying to breathe.

CHAPTER 19

We arrived in Berlin late in the evening, just in time for the Love Parade all-night party. On every second weekend of July since the wall fell, a million people from the four corners of the planet have been coming to the city for this giant rave. After spending a dozen hours on trains, Ihmre and I were pretty stiff and sore. We showered at the youth hostel, ate egg noodles, and took the subway for the Brandenburg Gate, where the wall came down.

Ihmre was wearing a long, multicoloured skirt splashed with yellow, white, purple, and blue, which caressed the mid-section of his calves most sensually. His eyes were heavily made up, and I had glued red stars under his eyebrows. The slit in his skirt showed the back of his knee and the beginning of his thigh. Ihmre had a musician's sense of rhythm. I rejoiced to see the nonchalant agility he flaunted. The swing of his hips was marvellously served by his androgynous charisma.

A sky of an apocalyptic pink was over our heads, as silky as kimono cloth. The statue of Victory spread its golden wings not far from us. A DJ was spinning drum'n'bass beats as if to amplify our sensual drives. Three placid policemen, sitting on a small hut that was serving as a public rest room, seemed mesmerized by a tall, Indian-type guy who was doing a balancing dance act on a lamp-post. A McDonald's crammed with people, rubbish everywhere, a church amputated of its spire, and several office towers formed a peaceful guard around us.

Quietly expanding, the ecstasy spread through me. Ihmre applied tiger balm on my temples, and I felt that the trip was beginning, I was going to experience a trip within a trip, I thought; I was grasping the full sense of the word "trip." I felt I was crying frozen razor blades and enjoying it. We were near some loudspeakers, and the sound and rhythms from them were building inside of me, in my veins and muscles, guiding my movements. The moment was coming, I sensed, when I'd want to touch and be touched. I had taken the drug of sensual craving and my senses would be wide awake, especially my sense of touch. I was aware of all this and found a beautiful paradox in it.

Suddenly, Ihmre began to rub my back with his bird-like hands and long, pianist's fingers. Two very blond boys, twins, each massaged one of my arms and hands, smiling at me. An Asiatic girl, seeing me in a trance this way, slipped two drops of a delicate oil behind my earlobes; they felt like ice cubes that tickled and made me shiver with pleasure. Ihmre bent and took hold of my lower legs, and the blond boys hoisted my upper body over their heads. Then I drifted, facing the statue of Victory, lying on a sea of hands, floating on hands that were holding me over the heads of a crowd. From where I was, all I could see were fingers pointing toward me and palms ready to take me and pass me along to other waiting hands.

The landing was as soft as could be; I was a human-shaped sponge leaving its marshmallow bed. Ihmre was right there with a pear-flavoured candy. We kissed, playing tongue-and-flavour games with the candy dancing back and forth from one mouth to the other. Our hands covered with gel touched and felt the other's, as if in warm, moving clay. The taste of fruit syrup was exploding in my chest, my legs were caught up in the electronic rhythms, behind my earlobes it was menthol winter and the music was all the better filtered, the more penetrating for it. There were smells of flowers, urine, sweat, cotton candy, and hamburgers. Berlin's big clock had stopped as if to banish time from the scene.

Someone came up behind me and with a firm grip began to massage my collarbones, throat, and neck. I shook my head and turned around to see who it was. The guy was a giant.

"*Nein, Nein, tut mir Leit, aber Nein.* Sorry, but no."

Ihmre placed himself behind me and with my back tight against his body I tried to put aside the memory of an assault on my person six months before. I had never told Ihmre the story and I felt a curious pride in having no one know about it but me.

The giant went away, showing his buttocks. He was wearing only a G-string and we burst out laughing to see his inhumanly overdeveloped Schwarzenegger build.

CHAPTER 20

To my great distress, I'm developing territorial reflexes, a "sense of property," the immoralist André Gide would say. It's embittering me, and I'm losing weight as a result–brooding destroys fats in me, kills lipids, leaves me at odds with my bones, dependent on the soft marrow.

"You took my hairbrush, Alex."

"Could be, I left mine at Isabelle's."

"Yes, but you could have been careful, it's missing some teeth."

"...."

"And those teeth are in the sink. Which means they're going to go down the drain and could block it."

Alexandre goes to clean the sink. I have no patience and am cross with myself for reacting this way. In fact, it hardly matters if he's taken my brush. He's becoming my whipping boy. He takes it all without a word and never gets mad. I try to study a bit, to read for my classes. The ink of the printing spreads, transformed into lazy fireworks.

"Alex, come here."

He hits his forehead against the upper doorframe. In this new apartment, the doorframes are lower than normal, and my brother must remember to duck his head. We laugh and he threatens to spank me with the brush while holding his forehead with the other hand. I massage his face.

"The doorframe wants to say it's sorry for mistreating you like that."

He brushes my hair and is amazed how long it is. I put on a scientific voice and explode some myths. Tradition has it that fear makes hair fall out or stand straight up on one's head. In my case, it seems to have lengthened it by ten centimetres or so.

I feel like eating Kentucky fried chicken. Alex is surprised and displays his dislike for the stuff. I explain that what I want is to munch on the crackly, salty skin and suck on the bones one by one. Don't care about the meat.

In the morning paper, Pierre Foglia writes, "I believe that wounded cats are like wounded people; they are dangerous because they know they can survive." I believe besides that they're that way because they've lost faith in the world around them. Knowing your survival is possible brings a strange joy, a primitive pride, an impression of raw strength in the best of cases. "Dangerous" seems a bit far-fetched to me. I'd say, perpetually distrustful, in a state of paranoid legitimate defence, with the fatigue that that entails. And fatigue changes personality for the worse.

While I'm waiting to be called, like at the doctor's, I read *La Presse.* At last the investigator appears, chubby and ruddy-faced, with a coffee in his hand which he hastens to offer me. He leads me past a drunkard under arrest who begins to talk about masturbation when he sees me coming. Three policemen flatten him against a wall, and the investigator runs to protect me. I'm angered by all this. First, why do they have victims walk down the same corridor as attackers? Second, I hate being rescued as if I were too weak to look after myself.

A procession of presumed young rapists of Latin blood parade before my red eyes. A number are dirty, unshaven, immoral-looking. It seems to me they deliberately stare at the window from where they know I'm studying them. There are a good fifty. A lot of assaulted girls in all, if you figure an average of two girls per rapist. I'm asked if I recognize one of them. I repeat that the attacker's face was hidden behind big sunglasses covering part of it and he was wearing a hood. I repeat that, apart from a brief confrontation, my eyes were blindfolded throughout the eternity of that half hour. It doesn't make any difference; in fifteen minutes max, the investigator will ask me the same question over again. As if, as the seconds ticked away, what I was saying was dissolving in the air, vanishing in weightless bubbles.

Six newcomers come in. One of them arouses an ambiguous feeling in me. In spite of all the contempt and distrust I feel for these guys, I know I would have turned around when this tall, slim one passed, with his tousled hair and his bright eyes and delicate nose. He leaves gracefully, like a cat.

"What's the matter?" the investigator asks.

"There are a lot of them, I find."

"They're the ones that meet the description and are 19 to 25 years old. Don't worry, it won't take much longer, there are just a few more, a dozen at most."

"Oh... it isn't really that I want to leave. But... I just figure there must have been a lot of girls assaulted when you get down to it. Why have you asked me to come and confirm when you found his wallet in the apartment of the third girl assaulted?"

"We have to do it, that's all. Compulsory confirmation before the trial. He's there," the fat fellow tells me. "The two other victims and your former house-mate have recognized him."

I want to be loyal to the others, I want to finger him, I want to recognize him. I want to more than anything.

"Now, Ariane, concentrate. We're going to show you six boys retained from the fifty. The two other victims have identified the same one. We're practically certain that he's the attacker. But we want your opinion."

I feel sick to my stomach. All of them are looking at me without seeing me. Of the six, three are too tall and I rule them out before I leave.

"It's one of the three others and that's all I can tell you. Can I go now?"

I wait for the métro at the Guy-Concordia station, suffering indiscreet scrutiny from three young Latinos sitting across from me on the opposite platform. More than ever, I'm convinced I must carry a weapon.

CHAPTER 21

The train left, on time as German trains do. Ihmre's feline silhouette was lost in the flow of people waving their hands on the station platform. We had spent our last moments together at Cuxhaven, right below Denmark, in a little inn near the North Sea. It was expensive and comfortable, and we disbursed the money we had left on luxury details: a bottle of Copenhagen wine, little sailing boat rides, meals of oysters and white fish.

The day before I left, a $20 Canadian bill fell out of my wallet. Ihmre thought it was English money at first. Explaining to a Czech in a creole that wavers between English and German how an English queen comes to be on Canadian money is as hard as doing a *101 Dalmations* puzzle. Not as hard, though, as explaining how an attacker comes to be in one's clothes closet.

This trip to Germany wasn't part of the plan. My brother, his girlfriend, and I had decided to go to France on a whim, with (among other sources) the money from the indemnity of victims of criminal acts. In March, four months after the attack, we were still in shock. I thought it would be a good thing not to have clothes closets to check out for a month. I was going to go to Sète with Alexandre and Isabelle. We took a train, then I saw this connection going to Stuttgart.

"I'm going to Germany," I said to Alex and Isa.

"You're not going all by yourself?"

"Yes, I'll be careful. I want to do this trip alone. I've been under your feet for five months; you'll have a chance to be alone together."

"Wait... Take this, at least. I don't think I'll need it anyway.

In a plastic bag, Isabelle had bundled up an old trench coat that reeked of mildew and a soft, very rumpled hat.

"But Isabelle, there's no room left in my baggage."

"Roll up the trench coat and squash the hat, that's all. It can be very useful to pass yourself off as a guy at times."

My brother's face was white. I had taken three German courses at junior college. My father would chew him out for letting me go. The German border officials stamped my passport. From the beginning I liked their handsome, angular faces, their distant respectfulness, and their silent grace.

I listened to jazz and was dying already of lonesomeness. Ihmre and I had promised to meet in New York the following year. We were going to get drunk in the little bars of Greenwich Village, listening to jazz, blues, whatever, and talking that creole language that only we understood. A conductor passed by and offered me a coffee... and a kleenex. Through my tears, I smiled at him, though I didn't see him.

My brother and Isabelle were waiting for me at Charles de Gaulle Airport. My eyes were white again, except perhaps for a little spiral-shaped vein in the corner of my right eye. Like the stamp in my passport that proved my visit to Germany, there was now a mark that confirmed my passage through another place with a great deal of history, the place of survivors.

Marie Hélène Poitras is a leader among the new generation of Quebec writers. She won the prestigious Prix Anne-Hébert in 2003 for her first novel, *Soudain le Minotaure,* the original French version of this book. Her work has also been short-listed for the *Prix de l'Académie (2003)* and the *Prix des Libraires (2006).* In 2006 she published a collection of short stories, *La Mort de Mignonne et autres histoires.* She is a journalist in the cultural field in general and music editor for the Montreal entertainment weekly *Voir.* She lives in Montreal.

Patricia Claxton has translated works by Gabrielle Roy, Jacques Godbout, and Nicole Brossard, among others. She has won two Governor General's Awards for Translation, a share (as translator) of the Drainie-Taylor Award for Biography, and numerous nominations. She lives in Montreal.